D0168027

ERASED

PUBLIC LIBRARIES OF SAGINAW

JUN 2 - 2009

ZAUEL MEMORIAL LIBRARY
3100 N. CENTER
SAGINAW, MI 48603

ERASED

JIM KRUSOE

PUBLIC LIBRARIES OF SAGINAW

JUN 2 - 2009

ZAUEL MEMORIAL LIBRARY
3100 N. CENTER
SAGINAW, MI 48603

Tin House Books

Copyright © 2009 Jim Krusoe

All rights reserved. No part of this book may be used or reproduced in any manner whatsoever without written permission from the publisher except in the case of brief quotations embodied in critical articles or reviews. For information, contact Tin House Books, 2601 NW Thurman St., Portland, OR 97210.

Published by Tin House Books, Portland, Oregon, and New York, New York Distributed to the trade by Publishers Group West, 1700 Fourth St., Berkeley, CA 94710, www.pgw.com

Library of Congress Cataloging-in-Publication Data

Krusoe, James.
Erased / by Jim Krusoe. — 1st U.S. ed.
   p. cm.
ISBN 978-0-9802436-7-3
I. Title.
PS3561.R873E73 2009
813'.54—dc22   2009009761

First U.S. edition 2009
Printed in the U.S.A.

Interior design by Laura Shaw Design, Inc.
www.tinhouse.com

FOR MY MOTHER

Darest thou now O soul,
Walk out with me toward the unknown region,
Where neither ground is for the feet nor any path to follow?

—WALT WHITMAN

My mother was a transcriber; that's what she did for a living, week in and week out. This was her routine: Once or twice a week she would take the bus downtown to the transcription service and put the tapes she was finished with, together with the computer disks on which she'd transcribed them, into a medium-sized cardboard box marked "Incoming" that the transcription service kept by the front door. "No Internet for them," she used to tell me with satisfaction in her voice, though no doubt that will change soon if it hasn't already.

Next, she would pour herself a cup of coffee from the pot in the corner of the office, put her purse down on the table, flop into a chair, and hang around for a few minutes to talk with Angela. Angela basically ran the place. Sometimes, if Angela was too busy to talk she would point to the phone she had pressed against her ear with her shoulder, wave good-bye, and mouth the words "next time." At least that's what my mother said. Then my mother would pick up new tapes from the box marked "Outgoing," also by the door, get back on the bus, and bring them home to her apartment. "It's a real grab bag," she used say. "Sometimes you get great ones that are easy to understand and fast to finish; at others you get some real stinkers." Angela was fair, of course, but a person didn't want to get on her bad side, either.

On the phone that night, my mother told me that earlier in the day she'd brought some new tapes home, and as usual inserted the first untranscribed one into her foot-pedal-activated, variable-speed tape player, and put on her headphones. Then she'd listened, typing what was said and who said it into her computer. After she finished the first transcription, she checked it on the screen for spelling and copied it to a disk. She said she'd done two more right afterward, and I knew that eventually, when the whole batch was completed, in about a week, she'd get back on the bus, drop the tapes, each in a separate envelope together with its disk, into the "Incoming" box, and hear another installment in the story of Angela's tragic life. Angela had a boyfriend who was a real horse's ass, my mother said, but Angela couldn't seem to shake him. "I told her he reminds me of your father, rest his soul," my mother said. "But that didn't seem to help."

You can see why I may not have been paying as much attention to the conversation as I might have.

The tapes were of lectures or interviews, usually from radio shows, and needed to be transcribed not so much because they were especially interesting or because they were going to be printed anytime soon in a book or magazine but for legal reasons in case, as sometimes happened, the originals got lost or needed to be examined quickly. "In other words," my mother used to say, "we're not talking high drama here, Theodore, only small claims court." So instead of containing great historical interviews with world leaders, et cetera, the tapes my mother copied were mostly filled with the voices of so-called experts droning on, sometimes with a semifamous personality thrown in. The names of these latter she would repeat to me with a note of pride in her voice, but usually she limited her conversation about the tapes' contents to the odd fact she found interesting.

That night, for example, my mother told me she'd just finished transcribing an interview with a scientist who claimed that mankind was destroying about eighty species of animals and plants and insects every single day—or maybe that was only the number for animals—I was just half listening because I was in bed by then and I was tired. Then there was a catch, or something, in her voice and she added, "Erased, just like that. As if they'd never been alive at all."

"Are you all right?" I asked, because I thought I heard a different tone than I was used to.

She told me she was fine, though, yes, she *was* feeling distressed at that moment. I imagined her lying in her bed in the apartment where she said she preferred to live instead of moving in with me (thank goodness). "Is everything OK with your apartment and your neighbors?" I asked.

I should add here that a part of me felt guilty because the neighborhood she lived in wasn't the best. It consisted of light industrial types of shops, places that bent metal or fabricated plastic, and was home to a few marginal businesses, like the Treasure Chest, the store she lived above. But on the other hand my mother was tough, and I hadn't asked her to pack up her belongings and come out to St. Nils to be with me. It was her idea. After all, until recently she'd spent my whole life not caring anything about where her only son lived or what was happening to him. So why, I wondered, should I feel the least bit guilty? I did, though.

Through the phone I could hear a car door slam every couple of minutes. It was the sound—I knew from having watched—of some guy pulling up to the Treasure Chest and running inside. Then, after a short while, the car door would slam again and the invisible door-slammer would drive off, carrying some box, some bag, some apparatus or another. I say "guy" because about ninety-nine out of a hundred customers of the Treasure Chest were men.

Then my mother's voice was back with a kind of strange quiver to it. "Theodore, if you're interested, I'll tell you. Actually a really odd thing *did* happen today," she said. "Though it's probably nothing."

I sat up in my bed. "Go ahead. I'm listening."

I pictured her at that hour. She would be lying in her own bed, holding the phone with her left hand. Her window would be open because she liked to sleep that way, and she was probably dressed in one of the white cotton nightgowns she favored; maybe she was even still in her bathrobe. As my mother talked, she would be looking at her right hand with its transcriber's fingers and short nails that she liked to cover with clear polish. It was a small thing, but I knew that she really enjoyed admiring her hands—one of the few places where I could measure her vanity. They were strong, practical hands, not showy, but well-shaped and smooth. She took good care of them. The rest of her was sturdy and no nonsense—"tough" I suppose some people might call her.

But she didn't sound tough then. Instead, my mother spoke softly, as if at that very moment she herself was transcribing what had happened earlier that day, or maybe was speaking it into an invisible microphone for another, imaginary transcriber to take down. "I had just gotten up from my desk—my 'work station' you know I call it—and walked over to the window to look down at the street below." Again, for a second I thought I could hear something entirely different in her voice. Was it fear? I pushed the thought away. Honestly, a part of me just wanted to stop talking and to sleep.

"Remember, this was only five or six hours ago," she told me. "It was evening and still light out, though naturally it was growing darker every minute, and while some people were coming home from work, others were heading out for what I suppose passes as pleasure these days: maybe dinner and a movie and a little dancing—who knows, Theodore— it's been a long time since I've done that myself and, really, that indoor stuff was never really my style."

I made a mental note that I should probably take her out to dinner one of these days. Then, out of nowhere, I started to feel really sad, as if I'd lost something I'd never find again, but couldn't say what it was. It wasn't the first time I'd felt like this, and I knew if I waited it would go away. I turned the TV on, with a picture but no sound, because that usually seemed to help. It showed a hockey game, men darting like angry wasps.

My mother continued, "So there they were, as I was saying—all those *lovers* hurrying to bed, those clerks hurrying home to their families, and those businessmen going who-knows-where, the funny secret look that people get when counting their money still plastered to their faces. It was still early enough for a few kids to be out on those horrible skateboards. I don't know why more of them aren't killed."

Skateboards were a sore point with my mother. I was born too long ago ever to have grown up with one, but didn't much care one way or another. Since when—I asked her in my mind—were *you* so interested in children?

I flipped the channel to a pantomime wrestling match

between two guys in sequins. My mother grew silent. When she spoke again her voice was even more different, and heavier. "So I was just looking out the window," she said, "and then out in the street a man stopped and looked at me. He was wearing a heavy, brown overcoat and carrying a dark leather bag. It wasn't exactly a briefcase," she added, "because it was lumpier and looked as if it had been designed to hold tools or maybe machine parts, and he didn't look like a businessman. And this man, Theodore, walked right up under my window, but instead of checking out the window of the Treasure Chest, as most people do, or avoiding it, this man stopped dead in his tracks. Then he raised his head and stared right at me, as if he knew me from somewhere."

"Maybe he did," I said. "Did he threaten you or harass you in any way? Do you think he was a stalker? I hope you got a good description of him and wrote it down, just in case. Maybe it's time for you to think about moving to a better neighborhood." I wished I hadn't said that part, but it was too late to take it back.

There was a silence as if she were thinking. After a bit she continued in that same weird voice, almost as if she'd been hypnotized, something I found hard to believe anyone could do to my mother. "Relax, Theodore. Your mom can take care of herself. But if you're asking what he looked like I only wish I could say. The fact is that right now, when I try to picture him, I can only remember that brown overcoat. And the bag. I'm sorry."

I waited for her to go on. This *was* a new voice. I had never heard her apologize for anything. Ever.

"And then," my mother said, "this man just stood there, and our eyes locked for at least a minute, maybe longer. 'You, Helen Bellefontaine,' he told me, 'are you listening to me?'

"I must have nodded or something," she told me, "because his voice became *quieter*, but at the same time—and I don't know how this is possible, Theodore—I could hear it even better. Then he said, 'You, Helen, who are looking down on me and all of us at this moment, thinking your thoughts, copying the words of others, has it ever occurred to you that you might not even be alive?'"

"What?" I said. "How would he know that you're a transcriber if he hadn't met you before?"

My mother said nothing. Surely, I thought, the man must have been someone she knew, someone she had talked to and then forgotten about, who was playing a bad joke. Except for Angela, though, and Ramon, who worked downstairs at the Treasure Chest, she never spoke of knowing anyone.

I was just about to mention this when she resumed. "Then the stranger's voice got even quieter. He said, 'Yes, Helen, I mean you. And despite your having a strong pulse and steady heartbeat, has it ever occurred to you for even one single moment that you might be dead, because not only for the living but also for the dead anything is possible? And if that sounds strange,' he said, 'think about it: Are you able to tell me right now what actual difference there would be between you being here and alive this very second and if you weren't but only thought you were? Answer that if you can with all the so-called wisdom you have culled from years of transcribing interviews, Helen Bellefontaine, and you truly will have hit the bull's-eye in the center of the target of human existence.'"

"He really said that? 'Wisdom culled from years'?"

"Can you imagine?" my mother said. "At first I thought he was an actor, but of course he said it. Do you think that being a transcriber I would have forgotten a speech like that? I even wrote it down afterward because it was creepy. Also, I have to say he was starting to piss me off."

It sounded like she was moving back to her old self then, so I felt a little better. "What did you answer?" I asked.

"I said nothing, of course. What can you say to someone who talks to you that way? I didn't say a word."

Then, my mother said, the stranger—whose hair she suddenly remembered might have been a medium brown—simply turned, walked around the corner, and disappeared. And it was only later, she told me, when she was still at the open window, looking out over where he'd been, that she realized it wasn't the kind of weather at all for such a heavy overcoat—it was much too warm—and whatever was in his bag couldn't have been tools because after he left she noticed there was a dark, moist spot on the pavement right where he'd been standing.

"Maybe," my mother said to me in an uncharacteristically tentative voice, "he was carrying a block of ice to a party."

I turned off the television and looked at the phone, which seemed to have grown heavy and impossibly cold in my hand. I imagined my mother had gotten up and was now sitting on the edge of her bed—or maybe she'd moved to a chair—holding her neat transcriber's hands out in front of her to make sure they were real. "But that's crazy," I told her.

My mother took a breath. "Tell me about it, Theodore, but you have to realize I was in shock. Honestly, it felt as though the man had struck me. I was sure I *was* alive, of course, but I started thinking: how exactly could such a thing be *proven*? I know, I could go to a doctor, of course," she said, and I could hear her thinking the process through. "So, suppose that tomorrow morning I did just that. Suppose I got on the phone and made an appointment, and then in a month or two, when I finally get to see one"—my mother had no health insurance plan, and something as simple as seeing a doctor was not so easy—"the doctor will tell me nothing's wrong and that I should take a vacation." She gave a laugh. "As if I can afford a vacation."

So much for falling asleep, I thought. "Excuse me for asking, but are you taking any new medication or anything like that?"

"Nope," my mother said. "But you tell me this please, and I'm not kidding: You know how in the past sometimes people used to be buried alive, and how it still happens now once in a while, though mostly in poorer countries. Then why can't the reverse also be true? Why can't someone who is actually dead be walking around right now? And if that person happens to be *me*, and a doctor really was able to confirm this, to sit me down and say, 'Yes, Helen, as a matter of fact you *are* dead. That stranger who spoke to you in front of your apartment a month or so ago was absolutely correct,' would I really want to know?

"Would *you*?" she asked.

I told her that was a good question.

"So, here's the thing, Ted," she continued, her voice lightening its way back to its old self. "I *know* I'm still the same person I was before the man called out to me. I know I'm fine—you don't have to worry—but there *was* something about him—about the fact he knew exactly where I lived and my name, too—that rattled me. I guess that's why I called you."

Then my mother made one of those laughs people use to show that everything's OK. "So, what do you think, Theodore? Am I alive, or am I like some device, say, an old fishfinder that a person keeps under the seat of his boat even though he has a new one that's much better in every way just in case he's out on the middle of the lake one day and the new one breaks, or he needs an extra part that he can take from the old one?"

"A fishfinder?" I said.

"You know," my mother answered. "Like radar, for finding fish. Or, come to think of it, maybe that guy was like a fishfinder, but instead of fish he finds people who are dead and don't know it, or maybe about to die, because, as he said, what's the difference, anyway?"

But even as I thought about what, if anything, I should do, my mother's voice changed again, this time into a one-of-the-guys tone she seemed to be able to produce at will. "Hang on for a minute, Theodore," she said. "Your mom is going to get up and pour herself a nice stiff glass of beer."

It was true—my mother liked her beer. The phone clunked as she set it on the table by her bed. I pictured her setting it down in order to pull on her red slippers, then picking up the phone again to carry it into the kitchen. Essentially, my mother's apartment consisted of three rooms: a living room, where she slept, a white-tiled bathroom, and, toward the back, a kitchen with a small light-blue table that caught the morning sun. The kitchen was where she usually ate her meals, and I knew that at that moment the blue table would be changing from blue to purple beneath the flashing red neon sign of the Treasure Chest, which advertised itself, in small yellow letters crammed beneath the larger ones, as "Your Family Center for Adult Entertainment." The Treasure Chest wasn't as large as a person would think a center for anything would be. But it was safe because, as my mother said, "The real sickos don't spend good money on this stuff, don't you worry."

I heard the pop of a beer can tab, and then she was back on the line again. "There," she said. "I can feel my pulse. Pulses don't lie, do they?"

I told her I didn't think they did, and there was more silence as she took a gulp (my mother wasn't someone who sipped her beer).

I didn't know what else to say. I thought that maybe if we stayed on the phone like that—her drinking beer, me listening—long enough, everything would rewind to where it had been before the stranger had called out. The recent past would be removed, and my mother would go back to being the exact same person she'd been earlier, back to when she was transcribing—indisputably alive, not special, not a saint, that was for sure, but back to being my mother, whoever *that* was—and I could get to sleep and go on with my life, as I had all those years without her. "Do you want me to come over for a while and stay with you?" I asked.

I got out of bed and walked to my own window. There was another long silence on the phone. The road outside my apartment was dark, and there weren't any cars going by. The street lamps across from me had burned out weeks ago, and the city still hadn't gotten around to fixing them.

My mother spoke. "Well, I think that beer has made me feel a lot better. You can always count on a beer. I'm fine now, Theodore. I know you have a successful business to run and all that. I'm going to try to get some sleep, and you should, too. So good night," she said. "I'll see you around. Thanks for listening to the worries of an old woman, even if she is your mother."

Do the dead sleep? Who can say? I imagined my mother lying there. Against her cheek would be her pink sheets, probably scratchy because she wasn't one for doing laundry, and no doubt she would be feeling the weight of her green wool blanket, as heavy as the dirt that covers a grave. She would watch the Treasure Chest's red strobe as it announced its location like a lighthouse in a choppy sea for anyone who needed the comfort of adult entertainment, or maybe, come to think of it, to warn lost sailors of rocks and danger. And then, thanks to the beer, she would begin to doze off, and maybe dream a little.

But I believe that was the first time I ever heard my mother call herself old.

2

THE NEXT MORNING
when I woke I was relieved to see that the world wasn't as
peculiar as it had seemed the night before. Outside on my
street, people were walking around carrying their rolled-
up newspapers, clutching their lunches in bags of stained
brown paper, and lugging briefcases, and although a certain frenetic resignation informed their gaits, at least they
believed in something. They believed they were alive. They
believed they had a future. And if they believed it, why
couldn't it also be true for my mother?

I went out for breakfast, and when I returned, there
was a message from my mother on the answering machine.
"Hello," she said, "I want to thank you for listening last
night. I feel a lot better now. I don't know what got into
me, Theodore, but if I said anything that upset you, you can

forget it. You know me. For some reason I wasn't my usual self."

Then a message announcing a new crisis in my business immediately followed my mother's. I sold expensive gardening implements, not the kind you see around every day, but the kind that are almost works of art. As you might expect, many of them were imported, so there were often supply problems, and while the business provided me with a comfortable living, a person had to stay on top of things. So I dealt with the first problem of the day (a hang-up at customs), and then another one came up, and another, and of course I had to fix those problems, so it wasn't until two full days later that I finally called my mother back to check on her.

But by then it was already too late.

Though maybe I'd better back up a bit.

Before I was born my father died in an accident after taking a part-time job at a car wash so he could make some extra money for my birth. Evidently, the accident was still a painful memory for my mother, because when I asked her about it years later, she only said that it was completely avoidable and he had been "an idiot." I was four when my mother left me with Linda, our neighbor, and went to Cleveland, Ohio, to restart her life with a man I never met. I somehow have the impression that money exchanged hands. So she stayed in Cleveland with whomever, and I stayed in St. Nils, and except for the occasional Christmas present and birthday card, I heard nothing from her the whole time I was growing up. For twenty years Linda had loved me, raised me, the only mother I knew, and, except for her occasional fits of depression during which she would sit in her bedroom for a day or two (I'd bring her chocolate milkshakes and blueberry muffins), Linda did the best she could. She packed my lunches, and came to school on parents' night, washed my clothes, and put out fresh ones every morning. She gave me a night-light because for a while I was afraid of the dark. When, for a stretch of a few months, I believed I would die if I changed my socks, she let it be.

In return I helped Linda with her small business of selling packages of what she explained was rare kelp to all the needy people who would come to our door at all hours of the day and night. The bell would ring, and if Linda was indisposed (something that happened more frequently as she got older) I would answer it to find some shaggy, red-eyed, health-food fanatic who simply could not wait for his or her next installment of healthy kelp. So I would run down to the basement, where Linda kept the stuff in Baggies, and bring however much they needed back upstairs. Then they would peel off some cash to pay for what they bought. "No credit" was Linda's policy. This would go on for a time, and then, when our supply was getting low Linda would phone someone, and in a couple days some captain of a Mexican fishing boat would show up at our door—usually at three or four in the morning—unload the bricks of kelp into the cellar, and collect a wad of *dinero*.

When I was in my twenties, Linda drowned on a trip to the beach with her club, the Foxy Seniors. She had pretty much shut down the kelp business, except for a few close friends, but it turned out that she had saved a surprising amount of money over the years, mostly in cash, and she

3 1390 01397 2052

bequeathed it all to me, along with the house. Given this sudden infusion of wealth, I made up my mind to start a small but reliable enterprise, one that wouldn't make me rich, but would provide a steady income and wouldn't let me down. At that point I had no idea where my real mother was, and I didn't much care.

One day, after weeding an area in the backyard where seeds from Linda's kelp plants had somehow managed to sprout despite the lack of a salty habitat, it came to me that it wouldn't be difficult to sell by mail high-quality gardening implements: shovels, trowels, pruners, and the like. I started small with natural elm-handled shovels and trowels, and over the years, thanks to a tasteful catalog, I built a loyal customer base based on the beauty and reliability of my products plus an ironclad guarantee (if there was something wrong, I replaced it, no questions asked). Actually the guarantee was pretty much only a gesture on my part because fewer than a quarter of the tools I sold were ever used; most were for display purposes only.

While I was spending my time in this fashion, building my business, unbeknown to me, my mother, back in Cleveland, had gotten work typing up two years' worth of transcripts from a local radio show called *Together Again*. The show, which aired Saturday afternoons, featured reunions of all sorts—from school chums to army buddies—but mother and child matchups were its specialty. As tape after tape entered her ears, my mother began to wonder what had ever happened to the son she had thrown overboard, albeit into good hands, so long ago. She said that things weren't going well in the rest of her life at that time, so with her modest wages hiring a private detective to find me was out of the question. I guess her point was that although she did nothing, the doors of her awareness had been knocked on, if not actually opened.

Then one day a catalog for expensive gardening implements arrived in her mailbox. It was addressed to "Occupant," and my mother, having no interest in gardening whatsoever, was about to toss it into the trash when she was struck by the picture of the pleasant-looking middle-aged owner of the business, his hand resting comfortably on a stainless-steel compost turner. She thought he looked familiar, and her curiosity was piqued. She went on to read the entire catalog and, when at last she made her way to the money-back guarantee, minus a small charge for shipping, and discovered beneath it the signature of Theodore Bellefontaine, she knew she had hit the jackpot. She contacted me with a letter on the back of the order form that began, "Dear Son."

A brief correspondence (missing even a halfhearted apology for her absence) ensued, but I assumed I'd never see her, until one day I got a call to come out to the airport and meet my mother's flight. She stepped off the plane wearing a blue down jacket and jeans, and her hair was pulled into a no-nonsense ponytail. "It's good to see you," she said, and shook my hand as if I were the guest. I suppose it *was* true— she had lived in St. Nils before I had.

"Don't feel sorry for yourself, Theodore," my mother said. "Linda was a great choice on my part. And besides," she added, alluding to her past as a sportswoman, "I had other fish to land."

A couple of weeks later, over a dinner of Italian food, she watched as I finished my spaghetti with red clam sauce. "I do believe you got your love of clams from me," she said, following that up with, "Those Cleveland winters are murder. I think I'll stay in St. Nils for a while."

I must have made a face of some kind, because she gave my hair a playful yank. "This isn't about you, Theodore. What's done is done. Get over it."

So although I helped her find her apartment above the Treasure Chest (she found the job transcribing on her own), it wasn't as if either of us felt we had to make up for what my mother referred to as "The Years That Got Away." We talked regularly on the phone, and I met with her about once a month for dinner, and sometimes afterward I would sit in her apartment to keep her company for a television show, but that was about it. As for her routine in St. Nils, besides a little gossip about Angela's love life, I knew next to nothing about how my mother spent her days. She had never spoken about health problems, for example, until that phone call, and I wasn't even sure that being told you were dead qualified as a problem if you felt all right.

My mother told me that she read, but I never saw any books around her place, so maybe she was one of those people who go to the library to do it, taking a book off a shelf, sitting down with it for a couple hours, and then putting it back when they've finished. Once, when I stopped to visit, I interrupted her watching a show on bass fishing. About her stay in Cleveland all those years she was largely silent, but sometimes when we were watching television or a movie together and someone made a reference to Cleveland, she would either nod in agreement or shake her head in disapproval as if to say, "That's not what it's like at all." My best guess was that something had taken place in that city that she didn't want to talk about. I wanted to believe that she harbored some deep hurt, some secret she did not want to reveal, even to me, her son, but honestly, it made me feel that she just didn't trust me.

Two days later, when I returned the call she'd made following the dead scare and got no answer, not even a machine, a question began to form in my mind, though only faintly. Maybe she had gone on that vacation she had talked about, I thought. She did have a history of dropping out of sight—even in St. Nils, where she'd disappear for a few days at a time and then return without an explanation. It was probably nothing, but it occurred to me that I'd never forgive myself if something had happened. It was true, she had left me for a long time—for most of my life if I were counting—but nonetheless I hated to imagine my doing that to anyone. I pictured her helpless in her kitchen, staring into space after having struck her head on the edge of the table, trying to reach the handle on the freezer door so she could raise herself up enough to reach in and pull out a tray of ice to moisten her parched lips, but being unable to reach it. If only she'd gotten one of those models with the freezer on the bottom, I thought. So before I started work that morning I went over to her apartment above the Treasure Chest and knocked at her door.

There was no answer.

It was likely she'd just run out to pick up a fresh batch of tapes and would be back in a minute or two, so I decided to use the key she'd given me to let myself in.

Once inside her apartment, I was glad in a way to see that my worst fears about finding her incapacitated or worse were not realized. My mother was nowhere to be seen but, on the other hand, the place was completely empty. There was no work station, no books, no radio, and no clothing at all. The furniture—her bed, her dresser, and her couch— was missing. Only the kitchen table and the stove that had come with the apartment were left, along with a stack of plastic bottles for recycling and in one corner a few leftover tapes stuffed into a plastic bag from the Treasure Chest. I was surprised, naturally, but it looked as though my mother had cleaned the place before she left. In other words: she hadn't been murdered or kidnapped. I picked up the bag and walked downstairs to find Ramon, the young clerk who worked the day shift, a time when things were mostly quiet in the family adult entertainment business. Besides Angela, Ramon was the only other friend I knew of that my mother had. Maybe he could tell me something.

Despite my reservations about the Treasure Chest as a place appropriate for anyone's mother (but how was I supposed to know what *real* mothers needed?), one of the reasons I hadn't protested too much over her decision to live above it was because of the presence of Ramon, who seemed to keep an eye on her. I liked him and, over the year or so my mother had lived there, I often stopped by to say hello either before or after my visits, during which times he used me to try out his sales pitch for any new merchandise that might have arrived. Ramon, who was in his midtwenties, favored skinny dark ties and white shirts over his top half, while over his bottom section he generally wore tan chinos and tennis shoes. His wholesome fashion sense extended to his attitude as well, and instead of the demeaning tone other clerks who worked there adopted toward their customers, he tended to treat the patrons of the Treasure Chest as if they were researchers into some mostly arcane, though vital, field of human behavior. My mother had told me he was dating the niece of Mr. Murk, her landlord and his boss. There was a sweetness to Ramon that shone through even the tawdry fog of heavy-breathing customers, and it wasn't unusual to find resting on the counter next to him a basket of homemade cookies or cupcakes that had been left by one of the very few women (or possibly some guy) who came to shop there. He seemed like a decent individual.

"Ted," he said as I walked into the store, "long time no see."

"Sorry to bother you," I told Ramon, "but do you have any idea what happened to my mother? I talked to her not long ago, and now she's gone. Her apartment was completely empty except for this"— I held out the Treasure Chest bag with the tapes inside. "Do you have any idea what's going on?"

"Oh," Ramon said, drawing out the sound. "Not really, but I assumed you knew. I wondered about it. One day she's here, and then a U-Haul with a couple guys wearing white jumpsuits shows up, and your mother leaves with them. She never told me why or where she was going, only that she'd be in touch. She didn't look upset or anything, if that helps, and she even baked me a half dozen cupcakes to say good-bye. She'd been talking about Cleveland lately, that's all I can tell you. Excuse me."

Ramon turned to help a man wearing something that looked like a black shower cap with spikes. My mother had baked farewell cupcakes for Ramon, I thought, and hadn't even bothered to let her own son know she was leaving. Clearly she had departed in a hurry, but why hadn't she written me a note or at least left a message on my answering machine? It was odd and upsetting, but I *was* relieved. Whatever had happened, she hadn't been kidnapped or anything. The idea of anyone kidnapping my mother made me smile despite myself. "Did she mention me at all in any of those conversations?" I asked.

Ramon finished with his customer. "Oh, I almost forgot," he said. "She said something about there being some unfinished business she needed to take care of, and that whatever it was, it was in Cleveland."

"Thanks," I said, more confused than ever, and went home. I felt cheated out of something, but I couldn't say what precisely. As a feeling it was getting to be all too familiar.

INTERVIEWER: So this experience of yours, as you're calling it, was what exactly?

GUEST: Well, it wasn't *my* experience, Lloyd, because technically speaking I was—you know—dead. So I guess it was more like someone else's experience mailed to me, or maybe e-mailed, or even a text message. With all this technology around these days I don't know what I'd call it. Honestly, it's still pretty confusing.

INTERVIEWER: And before you were dead you were?

GUEST: I was outside fixing my fuse box. One of the fuses had gotten jammed into the panel crooked and, I don't know—for some reason or another I was sticking a big orange-handled screwdriver into the fuse box to pry the fuse that was stuck in there back out, and if I'd thought about it for even a second I'm sure that I would have had more sense than to do something as boneheaded as that, but there I was—I had the screwdriver in my pocket already—so I just sort of automatically took it and shoved the tip in real good behind the fuse, and there it was.

INTERVIEWER: The tunnel?

GUEST: You're goddamned right, it was the tunnel, Lloyd, but not just any tunnel either. It was the exact tunnel from the football locker room to the field that I used to run through in my uniform the year I played high school varsity over twenty years ago. We had a nine and two record; I was a tight end, by the way.

INTERVIEWER: How can you be so sure it was the exact same tunnel?

GUEST: That's easy. Some genius had sprayed the words *Cugars Rule* on the cinder-block wall to my right, and there it was, even down to the fact that the genius had spelled Cougars C-U-G-A-R-S. Plus, the tunnel smelled of dirt and sweat and that sweet athletic liniment they used to put on us. I tell you, I loved that smell, Lloyd, nothing like it in this world, or, I guess, the other one, either. So in other words, I'd know that tunnel anywhere, but of course that day at the fuse box I wasn't wearing any football uniform, just an old pair of jeans I'd pulled on, and a T-shirt. I was barefoot, too, which was probably another mistake, and I was all alone; it was just me going out onto the field there that day all by myself like I was a Cougar again. That was the name of our team. The Cougars.

INTERVIEWER: So would you say you were going straight out to play on the fields of eternity?

GUEST: Maybe. But, as far as I could tell, it looked just like the stadium we used to play at in high school because I could see the grass outside the entrance, or the exit—whatever—was green and I could see part of a line running across it, you know, in chalk, like the fifty-yard line. Plus one other thing.

INTERVIEWER: And that was?

GUEST: The cheerleaders.

INTERVIEWER: You saw actual cheerleaders?

GUEST: Well, I didn't see them, exactly, but I could hear them out there talking. They weren't cheering yet because the game hadn't started, naturally, and I couldn't hear the words, but just the sounds, and they sounded the same as the way cheerleaders always sound, high-pitched girl talk, kind of soft and giggling, and sweet, and behind their talk I could hear the rustle of pom-poms, and then maybe a few thumps every so often when one of them would jump up and down to warm up followed by little huffs and puffs, and I could hear that, too.

INTERVIEWER: And how were you feeling at that point?

GUEST: How was I feeling? Lloyd, let me tell you, I was feeling great. I've always had a thing for cheerleaders, but I guess a lot of people do, you know, and there I was in the tunnel, not feeling like some dumb-ass forty-seven-year-old with a screwdriver still in his hand, but suddenly a sixteen-year-old all over again with lots of staying power, if you know what I mean, and nobody else around for competition, and those cheerleaders waiting out there just for me.

INTERVIEWER: And then?

GUEST: And then I opened my eyes and there's this guy who needs a shave real bad. He's chewing vanilla breath mints, which I appreciate, and wearing a blue jumpsuit as he pushes on my chest, which hurts like hell, by the way, and there are other guys around in blue jumpsuits, too, and even though I'm lying there looking up at the sky, you know, out of the bottoms of my eyes I can see a piece of yellow tape behind them, and in my hand, believe it or not, I'm still holding on to that stupid screwdriver.

INTERVIEWER: So?

GUEST: So I did what anybody would. I stuck it straight into the unshaved guy's shoulder to get him to back off, and he gives out this huge yell and everybody except him applauds—I suppose because I've come back to life—like the two of us are doing a magic trick of some kind, and he's holding his hand over where I got him and blood is coming out between his fingers. I don't think the screwdriver went in too deep because I was weak from being dead and all.

INTERVIEWER: And?

GUEST: And then when they strap me down this prick gives the straps a couple extra pulls to make sure I don't get up, although I can't say as I blame him and I am grateful and everything, so next they throw me into the ambulance and that's it: that was the last time I got a look at that tunnel.

INTERVIEWER: And those cheerleaders? Did you ever see them again?

GUEST: Afraid not, Lloyd. I guess they timed out or something.

3

SO AFTER that I returned home from the Treasure Chest and picked up the newspaper, only to receive a surprise of a different sort. It seemed that a woman in Connecticut had used one of the small handheld edgers I sold, one with a Damascus steel half-moon-shaped blade for making borders around window boxes and the like, to commit a particularly grisly crime. Within hours my phone began to ring, and for the next few days I was kept busy answering questions from the press and filling new orders, which had surged as a result of the publicity. In between calls I tried to think about my mother's sudden departure, but it wasn't easy. Then I had to drive out of state to visit a manufacturer whose rosewood-handled hedge clippers had suddenly developed a defective bolt and so were being returned by the dozens. After that I was gone for ten days to the western regional gardening convention. In other words, my life more or less reverted to what it had been about ninety-five percent of the time before my mother had appeared (or was it reappeared?). I'd mostly gotten over any hurt feelings I may have had about her leaving so abruptly and, though I wondered from time to time how she was doing in Cleveland, I honestly had to admit I didn't worry about it. We had tried to bond, my mom and I, or at least *I* had tried, but it just hadn't worked. Sometimes things were like that. That was life, after all. At least I'd gotten to meet my mother, and that was more than some people had.

About a month after I returned from a composting conference, an envelope arrived. It had no return address, and on one corner, beneath the postmark, which was Cleveland, someone had rested a can of beer or soda, the result being a yellowish half ring. Inside was a newspaper clipping from the *Cleveland Plain Dealer*, dated a couple of weeks earlier: "Fisherwoman Drowns in Pond." What followed was the briefest information: "Helen Bellefontaine . . . alone on a boat . . . Aurora Pond . . . services . . . cremation . . ." I felt as if I'd been kicked in the stomach. So that was that, I thought. There was no mention of me at all, or of any other survivors, for that matter.

Who had sent it, and why had they waited so long? I felt I probably ought to go to Cleveland, but when I got to the part about what purpose that would serve and what exactly I would do there so long after the fact, I stopped. I couldn't think of anything. Clearly I had missed not only most of my mother's life, as she had missed most of mine, but also the event of her death. Was I sad? Yes, sort of, but about what was hard to say. I suppose I was sad for a past that never existed, one I might have had, but lost. At least, I finally decided, my mother had died where she had wanted to be, out on the water, doing what she liked best, fishing. We should all be so lucky.

Then things finally settled down with my business, and I even started to think about taking a vacation for the first time ever. Maybe my mother's death *had* gotten to me in a way. I'd always carried around a few too many pounds, and it occurred to me that it might be a good idea to try out a sport—not fishing, that would be hers forever, but possibly something indoors, like billiards or bowling. I never did, however. Instead, things moved back into their old routines, and more time passed.

It was months later, on a Friday afternoon, when the phone rang and Ramon was on the line. "Your mother," he said, "sent you a postcard. You want to see it?"

"Ramon," I said, "my mother's dead. I'm sorry; I know I should have told you earlier, but she drowned in a boating accident."

"I'm sorry for your loss, Ted," Ramon said. "Your mom was a little rough around the edges, but I liked her. Anyway, I'm holding this card from her right now in my hand. Do you want me to toss it, or what?"

I thought about it. I assumed either she must have mailed it before her accident and it had gotten lost in the mail or someone had found it among her effects and finally passed it along. For a moment I wondered why she would send a card to the Treasure Chest instead of directly to her own son. After all, the notice of her death had come straight to me, but obviously someone other than my mother had sent it. If this card had been written before she died (and it *had* to have been) it was possible my address had gotten lost in her move; my mother was not the most organized individual. Plus, it was her habit, I knew, to kill two birds with one stone, and by sending it to the Treasure Chest she could pass on her greetings to Ramon as well. She knew that Ramon would call me, but she couldn't have been so sure I'd call Ramon. I was surprised to admit that this sort of behavior on her part still hurt a little.

"Don't throw it out," I told Ramon, "I'll stop by to pick it up," and I was halfway out the door when the phone rang again. It seemed that in an entirely different part of the country a copycat criminal had used the Damascus steel edger in a series of convenience store robberies, and so the calls from the press started up again. In between answering the phone and trying to head off a small movement to have the edger banned, or at least to require a license to buy one, I wasted the evening and much of the weekend. I thought about my mother's card, of course, but with her being dead it was clearly old news, so I didn't feel too bad. Should I have dropped everything and hurried straight to the Treasure Chest? Probably, but you have to remember our history, and, after all, she was no longer in this world.

It wasn't until three days later, after the weekend had passed, that I had a chance to stop by the store to see Ramon. It was odd, in a way, to look up at my mother's old apartment and see it still unrented, a vacancy sign in the window.

"Hey," Ramon said when I arrived. "There you are. I almost threw it out. I thought maybe you'd decided to blow your own mother off. That's cold, man."

I explained briefly about the edger business. "Wow," he said. "*You* sell *those*?" He handed me the postcard, and sure enough, there was my name, Theodore Bellefontaine, followed by "c/o the Treasure Chest."

"Theodore Bellefontaine," Ramon said. "At first I didn't even know that was you, but then I remembered the Cleveland thing. I didn't know that was your mom's last name— *que bonita*."

"Thanks," I said. "It was nice of you to call about it. I meant to come by right away, but, like I said, I've been swamped. Did it arrive on Friday, then?"

"Sure, the same day I called you," Ramon answered. "But no problem. Any time." He turned to watch a man in a trench coat practice opening it in front of the full-length mirror at the end of the store.

I flexed the postcard a few times in my hand. It seemed to be made not of paper but of some kind of plastic I'd never seen before, either one so new that it had just come out, or one so old that people had stopped using it. The side with my name on it was yellowed, as if it had been traveling for a long while. I looked at the postmark. It had been mailed only the previous week. "Something big has come up. I need to see you, Theodore, and soon," the message said, and I wondered what the something could have been. In any case, it was too late now, I thought. I turned the card over. The picture side showed a city in winter, with darkened skies and tall buildings like the frostbitten digits of an avalanche victim's rigid hand poking through a veil of snow. Far below the tips of the victim's metaphorical fingernails, down on the streets, were specks of men and women, scattered like pepper from a defective peppermill onto a white tablecloth. It wasn't yet night, and from somewhere behind the lens of the camera that had taken this photo (*was* it a photo?) the sun must have been setting, because a few of the buildings' windows were smeared with a sickly egg-yolky glow.

I turned the postcard back over again. What did it mean that it had been mailed only a week ago? In the upper left corner, right above the space where the sender was supposed to write a message, was printed in tiny, difficult-to-read letters: *Terminal Tower, Cleveland, Ohio, "Best Location in the Nation."*

"Take care," I told Ramon. "I'll keep in touch. Let me know if you hear anything." I took the bus back home.

It was just an ordinary postcard, I told myself, and yet as I sat in the third row back from the bus driver, a large fishy-smelling guy, I found myself picking it up and staring at the picture. It seemed important in a way I could not describe. In it, most of the shops had already closed, their sliding metal grates with forbidding diamond patterns pulled across or down their fronts to prevent smash-and-grab burglaries, while those still open looked as if they were about to close at any moment.

The bus stopped at my corner and I got off.

Once inside my house, I found a magnifying glass to take a better look. Beneath its lens, to my surprise, I discovered that what I'd at first mistaken for unusually healthy heads of hair on the people in the streets were actually caps made from fur or fuzzy yarn spun from natural fibers. The women who were outdoors on such a cold afternoon seemed to favor more elaborate head coverings, while the men chose styles that hearkened back to an era when hunting and trapping was the norm. Those children still out on the streets wore the caps of aviators, elves, or even Eskimos, as they trudged homeward in the gloom to their empty, unheated apartments after having been kept late at school for some small infraction, some tiny sign of disrespect to a teacher self-swollen by his or her vision of authority. The children's tiny noses were running from the cold, and their schoolwork had been haphazardly shoved into backpacks designed to mimic those carried by their elders on those grown-ups' beer-swilling camping trips to escape the city's noose, but which were revealed here as only impotent travesties of adult delusions, parodies of a never-to-be-attained freedom, though, surely, being only children, they could not know this yet, nor would it have been right that they should.

And inside those smaller packs, as if to top an already cruel joke, instead of their parents' granola bars, freeze-dried stroganoff, dry socks, butane-powered cookstoves, aluminum mess kits, and bags of desiccated fruit, were only what their elders called "tests"—childish versions of forms they would soon be filling out in earnest with ballpoint pens and roller balls in the adult world still to come: tax returns, driver's license applications, and, in time, their own sad medical histories attached to clipboards to be completed while they waited in the chairs of the offices of doctors who, in the long run, would never know enough to save them, no matter what they charged, though no doubt it would be plenty. But for now this all was only practice: these tests smudged with their innocent wrong answers, their Ds and Fs and tolerant C minuses inked in red on top, endlessly self-incriminating testimonials to their failures, to be taken home and hidden, the punishments for poor grades postponed but never completely deflected by the cotton wool of cartoon shows and sneaked adult videos borrowed from their parents' stash while their supposedly responsible progenitors were out of the house at PTA meetings, bowling clubs, and wine tastings. So these hopeless children plodded endlessly onward, their small red ears filled with the clanging sounds of the dismissal bell and their eyes blinded with the pathetic illusion of its freedom. Dismissal indeed, I thought: how rightly named, the dismissal bell for sure.

Cleveland, Ohio—I spoke the words to myself and they sounded strange. The very place my mother had gone when I was a child to start a new life for herself, the place where, having emerged briefly to come to St. Nils, she'd returned to in the end. Cleveland: the stage on which she had lived so much of her life and, at the same time, the mysterious curtain that had concealed so much about my mother. I moved the magnifying glass slightly to the left and wiped a thin smear of butter from its lens to see a woman out walking with the others, but apart from them, an unwed mother-to-be, judging by her lack of a wedding band and by—even beneath the bulk of her winter garments—what clearly was an advanced state of pregnancy.

But instead of the look of contentment that usually arrives with such a state, there was something else, more cloudy and uncertain, in this particular young woman's eyes. "See that patch of ice ahead? Should I avoid it by walking around it through the snowbank there, or just go straight across, right down the middle so that I might slip, causing a miscarriage?" she seemed to be debating beneath her breath. Thus the invisible good and bad angels who rested on the down-stuffed shoulders of her quilted ski jacket had been caught by the unseen photographer in midargument, the implication being, obviously, that while on the one hand, a slip might release her from the formidable task of raising a child by herself, a child whose father, himself the product of a deeply psychotic family history, clearly augured years of therapy for his at-present unborn son (and, yes, it *was* a boy, because even though she did not know this yet, the angels, given their spiritual ultrasound technique certainly did, just as they also knew that none-of-the-above mentioned years of therapy would ever make the least dent in the child's predisposition toward violence, which he had inherited from the man his mother would forever refer to as "The Miscreant" and from whom, if she had only thought about it for a moment or two at the time she met him while he was out on bail for stealing, of all things, a Volvo station wagon, she would have run like hell). But on the other hand, if she *did* slip and the child *was* lost, what then, and what kind of a person would she be to commit such an act so purposely? Was my own mother trying to tell me, by means of this postcard, that she herself had experienced such a dilemma when she had been pregnant with me?

On the other side of the card, beneath the caption for the picture, in the well-formed and precise handwriting I recognized as belonging to my mother, I reread her words. The card was signed, "Your mother, Helen."

Beneath that it said: "P.S. Tell Ramon to stay out of trouble."

There was no address, no phone number, not even a PO box. No way to have contacted her even if I'd gotten it while she was still alive. I put the uncanny postcard down. It was unsettling to receive it, but the mail system being what it was, not entirely unsurprising. Nonetheless, it brought with it a picture of one other thing: Cleveland, Ohio—a city that I had hardly been aware of, now heaved itself up before my imagination like an ancient snapping turtle that had swum up from the bottom of a pond onto a rotten log and lay before me, blinking in the sun.

Faced with all of this I did the only thing I could. I climbed into bed, shut my eyes, and prayed for pleasant dreams.

And so I remained in St. Nils tending to my business, which, thanks to even more garden-related crimes, was growing by leaps and bounds. In the most recent case the perpetrator had chosen one of the weed diggers I featured prominently in my catalog, a long and graceful tool with an elm handle that looked something like a screwdriver with a bent shaft notched at one end for grabbing stalks. The perp had shoved it into his victim's occipital cavity.

"Oh ho, the Emperor of Death," the owner of my local garden shop said when I stopped by to keep my finger on the pulse of what was happening at street level. Then he ducked down behind his counter as if I were going to attack. "Please don't kill me."

"It's not funny," I said, but of course that only added fuel to his wit, such as it was. "It's 'Arbor Day Three,'" he said.

Nor did things stop there. The possibly deliberate choice of murder weapons in these crimes and the fact that they were all available through my catalog became the subject of a superficial article in an Internet blog devoted to hideous crimes, which in turn caused business to increase so much that I had to hire an assistant, a recent MBA grad named Marty, and of course training him took more time as well.

Anyway, it was about three months after I had gotten that freak postcard from my mother, and I was staying late at work, just finishing up paying a stack of bills to my suppliers, when I got another call from Ramon. "Theodore, I don't know if you care," he said, "but this is getting really strange. Believe it or not, another postcard from your mother just arrived for you at the Treasure Chest. Do you want to stop by and pick it up, or shall I toss it? It's probably just some crank, right? I mean, it's not like there's anything you can do, her being dead and all."

But this time felt different; this time I felt guilty for having done nothing. I felt guilty for abandoning my mother just as she had abandoned me. I was not like her, I told myself. This time I was at the Treasure Chest within the hour.

The second card was completely different from the first one. It wasn't of a cityscape, or of much of anything as far as I could see. It seemed to be a picture of some shiny brown substance, maybe chocolate pudding, or water, or even motor oil. I stared at it, trying to find a clue as to what it was. The only thing I could figure out, after staring for about a minute, was that underneath the surface of whatever it was there might be a bulge—maybe a seal or a muskrat or an otter, but it was impossible to be sure. The camera it had been taken with must have been a cheap one, and though there was something that might have been air bubbles, it could have been water damage because Card Number Two looked as if it had gotten really wet at one time or another. It was made of the same weird plastic as the first one, but the message on the other side was even shorter: "Theodore," and then the words "I'm not kidding." The "I'm not kidding" was underlined.

There was still no address, or phone, or any way to contact her.

As I held the card in my hand, I could feel a strange warmth from it, as if it were a living thing that possessed an urgency of its own. This time something had changed in me. No matter how little information I had, no matter how few clues I had to guide me (none) it was clear I had to go. Marty knew enough to run the business, and besides, we'd be in touch by phone and the Internet. I called an airline, booked a flight, packed my bags, and left the town where I had been raised to head for Cleveland. Whatever mystery lay there, I would not abandon my mother as she had me. Even if this whole trip came to nothing, I would have made the effort. I would act better than my mother had. My mother would have walked away. I would not do that.

⟨ **4** ⟩

IT WAS LATE SUMMER,
nearly fall, when I finally arrived in Cleveland, and the very
first thing I learned was that contrary to the small, discouraged, frozen image of the city in winter that had lodged in
my mind thanks to that first ominous postcard, late summer in Cleveland was a different world entirely.

From the moment my plane touched down on the pleas-
antly scented tarmac of Hopkins Airport, I could see all
around me crowds of vibrant, happy people, of all races,
creeds, and ethnicities, pouring out sweat from healthy
pores, writing in the very ink of their perspiration an ode to
life that instantly published itself in the underarms of their
sheer blouses and across the backs of their plain work shirts
until, collectively, each blouse and shirt joined together to
become an entire manuscript of poetry, a hardback edition
or a better-quality paperback. It was as if the snow depicted

on that first mysterious postcard had somehow been re-absorbed by these perpetually moist inhabitants who, unlike other folk, must have been made not only of flesh and blood but also of some sort of spongelike supplement that, in joyous bursts and slow trickles, released its hidden store of moisture before my very eyes.

And if Paris had been dubbed the "City of Light" and Chicago the "City of Broad Shoulders," then, surely, seeing its inhabitants up close for the first time, I thought that Cleveland must be—though to my knowledge no one had yet bothered to name it such—the "City of Noble Foreheads," for the simple reason that each inhabitant, no matter what race or culture, nationality, or social class—whether man, woman, or child—sported a brow so wide and untroubled as to make me, whose forehead always was and still remains unusually narrow, feel, as I walked up and down the sidewalks of Cleveland, like a slightly sad and overweight borzoi among so many jolly mastiffs and pit bulls.

Perhaps, I speculated, there was some mysterious ingredient in the local drinking water, some calcium salt from long-dissolved limestone deposits that, when taken into the human body, shot straight up (maybe it was calcium carbonate) to the front part of the skull, resulting in an unusually large brain vault for those children lucky enough to be raised with that supply of life-giving fluid. And what brains they turned out to be!

Because yes, it was true, I *had* read the words printed on that first postcard my mother had sent me, proclaiming Cleveland as the "Best Location in the Nation," but perhaps because of the unpleasant clunk of its rhyme, I had passed it off as just another mendacious slogan created to lure new business to the rust belt of America. However, now that I was actually seeing this city for myself in all its summertime splendor, all I could think was, "Ted Bellefontaine, how could you have been so mistaken? You should be ashamed of yourself." For Cleveland's towering skyscrapers (which on that first, misleading postcard had seemed only narrow and forbidding conduits of doom), clearly had not only survived the snows undamaged but, six or seven months later, were stuffed to the brim with hundreds, probably thousands, of hard-working, deep-thinking (and I believe I already mentioned heavily perspiring) individuals who, like ants in a colony that had survived a recent winter (did ants hibernate?), now raced back and forth to repair the damage of the cold days gone by, hurrying to buttress their foundations against future snows in order to keep safe their knowledge—and believe me, there was plenty—from their future near disasters.

So the city's busy folk hurried by, intent and yet also humble in the face of the tasks that lay before them, carrying their precious books, their sheaves of rolled-up architectural drawings, and their recently dried paintings in both acrylic and oil, because, yes, Cleveland had turned out to be not only a city of thinkers of a practical and intellectual sort but also a place where nearly every inhabitant was encouraged to practice at least one of the "fine" arts, whether it be painting, drama, sculpture, music, poetry, or dance, often combining several of them at once in unusual and surprising ways: painted dancers, rhyming sculpture (not the best idea, as it turned out), musical comedy, and even musical tragedy.

Wherever I went I looked and wondered. Where had those sad and hopeless children of that winter postcard gone? Was it possible the *real* Clevelanders hid out of sight during those snowy months and replaced themselves with a race of inferior tourists, possibly on loan from some country in the Eastern Bloc or the slums of some other city—Chicago, for example? For in the place of those pedagogically challenged pupils tragically captured on that first postcard was a swarm of small scholars, little Isaac Newtons, pint-sized Copernici, each sporting attractive eyeglass frames filled with exactly the sort of corrective lenses that might be prescribed for those who had studied hard and late at night on those endless winter evenings. (Seeing their insatiable thirst for knowledge, who could blame them?) Now, even in late summer, with school long out of session, these smallest Clevelanders ambulated through the streets of their city carrying, in addition to their Little League bats, regulation soccer balls, and swim team Speedos, stacks of texts on every subject: medicine, agronomy, astrophysics, astrology, genetic engineering, the culinary sciences, and more.

I stared at them and they stared back at me. "Here I am," each small face seemed to say. "I am ready to face the future unafraid, because I have been trained by the best minds in Cleveland. I have had demonstrated to me, even at my early age, the full extent of my intellectual potential, starting from A and ending with Z. Furthermore, Mister, it is only in that same potential, not in any mind-numbing mass hypnosis of religion or phantasm of the so-called media and the state working in subtle collusion, in which I shall place my boundless optimism and faith for my own future and the future of this great city."

What would it have been like if *I* had been lucky enough to be raised here with a real father and mother, instead of back in St. Nils inside the little clapboard house with—the more I thought about it—the loving but possibly in-violation-of-the-endangered-kelp-act Miss Linda? I involuntarily touched my narrow forehead. What would my life have been like if my mother had taken me along with her all those many years ago?

It was hard to say.

And not only were these children different from those in that earlier snowy scene, but instead of the swarms of distressed unmarried moms I had expected to find, in real life, so to speak, I saw practically nothing but contented, massively foreheaded couples walking hand in hand as they carried their books, stacks of their favorite CDs, pieces of sculpture, even loaves of fresh-baked bread, meeting and greeting other couples like themselves as well as scores of carefree singles, the members of this latter demographic striding confidently toward whatever lives they envisioned living, evidently having obtained enough insight through psychotherapy to explain the underlying reasons for his and her current unmarried state to relax and, possibly, as a bonus, also be free of whatever self-destructive impulses or neurotic drives that might otherwise have brought them to the situation so dramatically portrayed on that wintry postcard. Because far from searching for ways to abort unwanted fetuses, these tanned and confident individuals stood, or walked, or hummed by on bicycles, or skateboards, or in-line skates, and instead searched the crowd in the secure knowledge that somewhere out there, in some bar or library or mosh pit, there was a person just as smart and confident and good-looking as they were: for every Jill a Jack, for every square peg a square hole, for every deviation under the sun—and what a glorious day it was—a fellow deviant. "Don't worry, pal," their confident air seemed to reassure anyone who cared to ask, "if my exact match is not actually here with me at this very minute, then he or she will appear when the time is right. Take things in your stride, friend. Go with the flow. *Namaste.*"

It was easy to see why my mother had felt the need to return so strongly that she just packed everything up in one day and left. But *why* hadn't she told me she was leaving, or, for that matter, why had she kept secret the fact that such a paradise existed? Why didn't everyone know about this place? I asked myself. But also, and more importantly, now that I had arrived, what should I actually do? I wasn't even certain if the person I was searching for was alive or dead. Where should I start to find some trace of my mother?

I checked into a hotel room. Because my funds were limited, I knew that the following day I would need to find a less expensive launching pad for my search, but for that first night a hotel room would be fine. It was and more: it came with a complimentary cup of chamomile tea, a vanilla wafer, and even a CD of lullabies from around the world—and when I woke it was morning.

The next day I took advantage of a contact I'd made back in St. Nils when I had picked up that second postcard and Ramon must have seen the desperation in my eyes. "It so happens," he'd said, "that I have a cousin, Raul, who works in a store that carries a similar inventory as the Chest. It's called Love Hurts, and when I spoke to him just the other day, Raul mentioned that Love Hurts has a room for rent above it at a price a lot less than what we were charging your mom. If you decide to go there for a visit, you should look him up. If you like, I can give him a call and tell him to hold it for you until you arrive." I told Ramon I'd be grateful.

As soon as I finished the continental breakfast (a peculiar-looking donut, jam, fresh fruit, and coffee) that came with my room, I dressed, found Love Hurts, and it turned out Raul was expecting me. Love Hurts was a bigger store than the Treasure Chest, and this meant that the apartment above it was more spacious than my mother's had been, with a separate bedroom in addition to a larger kitchen, bathroom, and walk-in closet. It was graciously furnished in Eastern European decor, with smooth dark dressers and heavy overstuffed chairs, and had, hanging on one wall, a painting of a brownish horse. "It's an original oil," Raul told me proudly, and when I examined it I was pleased to make out several of the brush strokes, though they were hardened by evaporation and cracked by time. The horse stood in a pasture, his head poking over a wooden fence. His broad forehead (he must have been a native) faced the viewer with a level and intelligent gaze, as if to say, "Welcome, Seeker. You are not alone here, because we are in this together.

Your mistakes shall be my mistakes; likewise, I shall share in your successes. Here, if you will but be patient, observant, and keep an open heart to the myriad possibilities of your future, you will find exactly what you need."

The floors of the apartment were mostly covered by linoleum of an attractive red swirled pattern, and at the edges where one room led into the next, shiny silver strips of metal had been screwed down tight to hold the linoleum and prevent a person from tripping. The only exception to the linoleum motif was in the living room, which had faded wooden floorboards mostly covered by a large rug made from torn-up rags, skillfully formed into a near oval. The rug was predominantly blue, with some green and an occasional spot of brown. It gave the impression of looking into a puddle into which several clumps of leaves had fallen.

The windows had white curtains, and the light that streamed in gave the place a bright and cheerful feeling. As yet another benefit, my view overlooked the stately, light-brown Cuyahoga River, and on any given day, but especially on weekends, I could look out upon boats full of punters dressed in white, fishermen wearing hats festooned with lures, amid a blend of wild and domestic ducks, and even an occasional water-skier waving gaily as he capsized the punters' long, narrow boats and frightened the birds.

I told Raul I'd take it for a month and then let him know after that.

Cleveland, I soon learned, sported both a first-class symphony and art museum, as well as a hall of fame for burnt-out rockers and countless small, somewhat shabby cafés where one could spend an inexpensive afternoon watching writers write and artists (this included nearly everybody) sketch, while in the background musicians strummed tastefully on acoustic guitars or banjos, or, lacking instruments, whistled. And speaking of "tasteful," the specialty of the town appeared to be an enormous chewy donut, similar to the one I had gotten at my first continental breakfast at the hotel. It was a part of the city's aforementioned Eastern European heritage, was about the size of a potato, and was served plain or filled with jelly, but in either case came lightly dusted with powdered sugar. In no time I found that six or seven were a meal in themselves, albeit not a very healthy one.

So in my first week of searching for my mother, dead or not, I visited those cafés, ate their donuts (putting on a few pounds in the process), and sipped my coffee. I checked the coroner's office and went to the office of the newspaper, the *Plain Dealer*, in search of the reporter who had covered the original story of my mother's death. (He had long since disappeared into alcoholic rehab, and the paper's records for such things were a hopeless mess.) I called around to various transcription services to see if my mother had visited any of them in the weeks before she died. As far as I could tell, she had not. I checked the voter registration rolls, the utility companies, and the motor vehicles department. According to all of them, my mother had left no trace of her life in Cleveland. I talked to the police. Their report concerning her death was a mini-masterpiece of concision, with a large coffee stain having obliterated the most important parts.

"But look at this," I said as I showed my mother's first postcard to the officer in charge of police department records. He looked at it, turned it from one side to the other, then shrugged and handed it back. "That's an unusual material you have there," he said. "Is it something new?"

I bought a map and located Aurora Pond, the scene of my mother's final accident, but could not yet bring myself to take a trip out to see it.

I showed the two postcards to the people at the main post office. They only shook their heads and, when I mentioned the delays in delivery, got very defensive and were of no help at all.

I kept in daily touch with my business, and, if I could believe Marty, it was booming.

tape two

INTERVIEWER: So, Brute, how long did you say you've been incarcerated here at the state prison since the actual event we are about to speak of took place?

GUEST: I'm counting thirty-six years so far, and, with a little help from my buddy, Jesus, I'm figuring I have another thirty-six still to go.

INTERVIEWER: Serving a sentence for . . .?

GUEST: For eight consecutive life terms. That means . . .

INTERVIEWER: Thanks. I'm only too aware of what *consecutive* means.

GUEST: Well, OK. A lot of people, especially your buddies in the liberal media, don't. Anyway, my attorney tried to get all those little life terms changed to just one big life term without parole, but no, the smart-asses had to go and do it the hard way. Eight.

INTERVIEWER: And this was for?

GUEST: Come on, don't play dumb with me, asshole. You know real well what they're for. You wouldn't be here interviewing me with that fancy tape recorder if you didn't know.

INTERVIEWER: You're correct, of course, Brute, but I'm asking for the listeners, not me, and I must say that at this moment—and here I'm also speaking on behalf of the listeners so they can begin to form a picture of the way you appear—you don't really look a whole lot like a man of the cloth with all those tattoos, and those biceps of yours, which must measure, what—eighteen or twenty inches?

GUEST: Well now, I suppose that depends on exactly what you think a man of the cloth should look like, don't it, Sparky? You been around God much?

INTERVIEWER: (silence)

GUEST: I didn't think so. Fucking sinner. And just for the record they are twenty-three inches.

INTERVIEWER: Excuse me. And those eight consecutive life sentences are for?

GUEST: So, OK. You want me to say it? Maybe it will make you feel good or something? Here it goes: A while ago I set this house on fire and eight people died. And four of the ones who burned up just happened to be little kids. Does that make you happy?

INTERVIEWER: And they were your neighbors?

GUEST: Well, sort of. They'd only moved into my neighborhood a couple months earlier from some left-wing place like Oregon or Massachusetts, so we weren't exactly neighbors. Besides, I was living there first, and it wasn't as though I'd forced them to move next door to me or anything.

INTERVIEWER: And you burned their house because?

GUEST: They were starting to piss me off.

INTERVIEWER: Piss you off, Brute?

GUEST: You know. With their bumper stickers and empty bottles of wine from France in the trash. That's how I was in those days before I found Jesus. I ain't proud of it, but if somebody pissed me off I'd just torch them or something.

INTERVIEWER: And now?

GUEST: Now I think of all the people who must have pissed Jesus off, and believe me, there would have been plenty back in those days, but he never did nothing at all. Of course, that's because he was Jesus, and not me.

INTERVIEWER: I see. And you were saying when we spoke earlier that it was the experience of nearly dying that converted you to take Christ as your personal savior.

GUEST: Yes, it was. Just like Jesus died and came back from the dead, so did I. That's how I first started to relate, you see.

INTERVIEWER: And would you care to describe your experience to us now, Brute?

GUEST: No problem. I'm on laundry detail—you know, taking everybody's dirty clothes to the laundry—and, believe me, clothes can smell really nasty in a maximum-security prison.

INTERVIEWER: I hadn't thought of that. I suppose they can.

GUEST: What do you mean, you "suppose"? I'm telling you they can, dickhead. This isn't a debate, you understand? Anyway, there I am, shoveling everybody's stinking shirts, and underwear, and trousers—socks too, they're the worst—down into the laundry chute, when who do I see but this guy I stiffed out of a carton of smokes a couple days earlier, and he's coming at me with a shiv. That's a knife, for your information.

INTERVIEWER: I know what a shiv is, but thanks for making it clear to our listeners.

GUEST: So there's two choices I have, right? Either stay there and fight the guy and probably get cut up in the process or go down the chute, dickhead, so that's the one I choose. But he gets smart and keeps shoveling dirty clothes in on top of me, trying to suffocate me is what I think, and he almost succeeds because there's no air down there, and then I pass out so I can't see anything. And that's all I remember until suddenly there's a light, and I'm looking up at Jesus.

INTERVIEWER: You actually saw Jesus?

GUEST: Sure. Jesus Lopez. In for carjacking and kidnapping—twenty to life. He's standing there and he says, "Hey man, get the fuck up or do I have to kick you?" So I do, and that's the exact minute I was converted from my former ways. I figured it was a sign if there ever was one, like the real Jesus was saying he was sorry because he was tied up at the moment, maybe with his mom or someone, but he wanted me to think about him anyway, so he sent Jesus Lopez instead.

INTERVIEWER: What an inspiring story. I actually hate to ask this, but I have to. That guy with the shiv, did you ever wind up doing anything to him?

GUEST: That's the great part. Naturally, I was going to at first, and then I started thinking that Jesus had lots of reasons to be pissed off, too, what with the being put on the cross, and still he never did anything, and even when he came back and rolled the stone from his grave he made sure that nobody who could have gotten hurt was standing in front of it. That's my favorite part. It's in the Bible, but most people forget it, how Jesus looked through that stone first with his X-ray vision to be sure that nobody was standing on the other side before he rolled it away.

INTERVIEWER: So you were going to turn the other cheek. And then?

GUEST: And then the next day, maybe it's a Wednesday, I see the guy who had the shiv out in the yard, so I walk up to him and I figure I'll ask if he's still feeling pissed off, and if he says no, I'll say to him, "God bless."

INTERVIEWER: And he said no?

GUEST: Actually he said yes, so I popped him a couple times in the back of the head when the guard had his back turned, and that way he had something to be pissed about. But—and here's the thing—I didn't kill him or anything like that.

INTERVIEWER: I see what you mean. Thank you.

GUEST: Hey, no problem, dickhead. God bless.

5

TO SUM THINGS UP:
though I was lucky to be in Cleveland with its tree-lined streets and well-shaped concrete curbs, I had made zero progress regarding the whereabouts of my mother, dead or (and this was truly unlikely) alive.

"Theodore," I kept telling myself, "you need a *real* plan." But the best plan I could come up with was to visit various souvenir stands and stationery stores to see if I could find any cards with that same uncanny picture of the city in winter and ask the bored clerks who sold them if they possibly remembered anyone who had bought a card like that. As for asking about for the second card, the brownish blur, I didn't think I should bother. Even the first one was a long shot. I found cards with pictures of the zoo, members of the Cleveland Indians baseball team, various musicians from the symphony, pieces of the art museum's collection, and, in Love Hurts, photographs of a whole variety of people looking either extremely uncomfortable or the opposite, but never even a single scene of Cleveland with any snow at all. Was it possible that my mother, dead or alive, hadn't really needed me here at all but, following our discussion regarding vacations, had only summoned me here to enjoy myself? It *was* possible, but it didn't sound like my mother.

In any case, I had nearly three weeks left on the lease to my apartment, and so to pass my time while I formulated another strategy, I took a painting class, where I learned not only various techniques of watercolors and oils but also impasto, chiaroscuro, and foreshortening. The days went by. Encouraged by my success in painting I tried a course in fiction, though that turned out to be a dud, and after a week I dropped out and replaced it with a sculpting class that made all the difference to my sense of purpose. Not only did it teach me several techniques I found useful in emergency household repairs, but, as I carried my unfinished work with me around the city on the advice of my teacher, Sunshine, so I could "live with it," I felt practically like a native in the company of so many more-accomplished Clevelanders carrying their own busts of plaster of paris and papier-mâché.

Sunshine was a large woman, and every so often she would pick up a fifty-pound box of clay and press it above her head a few times "to keep in shape," as she put it. It was after seeing my first effort, a head of Medusa on which the snakes kept breaking off so that in the end they looked like curlers, that Sunshine had turned to me. "You obviously have some serious issues with women, Theodore," she said, "but I don't hold it against you because, as is so often the case in the world of art, I believe you may be able to use them to your advantage. I'd suggest that you sign up for lessons several times a week. It just so happens I have a special going on, which I'd advise you to take advantage of."

I did, and Raul said he was happy to extend the lease on my apartment for another month. So I searched for my mother and sculpted, each day a blend of souvenir shops (there were *a lot* of them) and EZ Sculpt, but even as I made progress in my sculpting I found myself getting discouraged with the searching business.

Then I got a lucky break. One particularly beautiful cloudy Cleveland afternoon in early October I was on my way to the library to do some more or less last-ditch research to try to discover if, back when my mother had first left me to come to Cleveland, her name had ever appeared in the newspaper (I didn't really know how that would help me, but I was desperate for the slightest clue) and was carrying with me a large bust of Athena on which the nostrils had come together by accident to form one giant nostril. The problem I was trying to solve—in addition to my mother's whereabouts—was whether the single nostril was too noticeable to leave, or, if I had to fix it, how?

So there I was walking in the direction of the library, alternatively picturing in my mind the statue with the one large nostril, and then with two, trying to decide which was more true to the spirit of the Goddess of Wisdom, when I stepped on a piece of gum that, as it adhered to the springy sole of my tennis shoe, began to throw my normally somewhat awkward stride completely off balance, and I was wondering what I could use to scrape it off when I happened to spot a nearby Popsicle stick that someone had thoughtlessly—but in this case helpfully—left lying on the ground, so I walked over and picked it up. Standing on one foot, still holding the bust of Athena under my left arm, I raised my right shoe high enough that I could see its sole, complete with the offending bright purple and very fresh wad of gum. Using the end of the stick, I began to pry it off. The gum, however, didn't release itself as easily as I thought it would, and as I bent farther, the next thing I knew I had lost my balance, and my head (my own, not Athena's) was aimed straight for the edge of a nearby concrete water fountain.

When I came to, the first thing I saw was a pigeon pecking the gum off the sole of my shoe. I let it continue. The second thing was a tall, slender, though muscular woman in her midthirties with spiked orange hair and a metal thing through her upper lip. She was impressive, and possibly even more so for the tattoo on her right arm that, even as groggy as I was, appeared to be of a rottweiler eating its own intestines.

"You clean," I heard her say though my ringing ears.

"What?" I said.

She repeated the phrase several times, until I finally understood that she was neither making an observation about my personal hygiene nor commending me for my lack of a drug habit. She was only telling me her name, which I eventually understood to be Uleene.

"Are you OK?" she asked. "I was watching you standing there, man, wondering what the hell exactly you were doing, and then all of a sudden you fall over just like that. Do you have low blood sugar or something? I know you're not exactly starving, but there's a direct relation between low blood sugar and overeating in that high insulin levels often create an artificial craving for food; I'm talking extra pounds." She poked me gently in my stomach with her foot. "Say, that's a good-looking bust of Athena. Is it some kind of fountain where a person can attach a hose or something there in front beneath her nose?"

Uleene's teeth, I noticed, were badly chipped, as if she had lived for a time on a diet of rocks. Even in my semiconscious state I could see there was an unusual energy about this woman, a blend of the sincere and passionate, the helpful yet diffident, full of a sort of smoldering intimacy combined with practical information of a medical nature. I looked at her ripe breasts, her slender waist, her freshly bruised knuckles and torn clothing. She reminded me of something, but what? And then it came to me: the poster for one of my all-time favorite movies, *Rampaging Biker Girls*, although the poster had featured not one but three women: one African American, one Asian, and an albino, all with their clothing ripped in a provocative manner. Surprisingly, however—and in contrast with the woman now standing above me—none of the three on the poster had even the tiniest visible tattoo.

I attempted to speak and my mouth seemed far away.

"Honey, are you there?" she said. Then, somehow sensing that no response was immediately forthcoming, she added, "My full name is Uleene Trail, and I'm thinking that it is your blood sugar level because I don't usually pick up strangers in the park, but, honestly, I'm a sucker for a helpless guy, and with that fresh head wound, you bring out the mother in me. How about if I buy you a . . . *something something . . .*"—her voice faded for a second or two—"fruit drink from a stand not far from here? Or, if you are feeling a bit stronger, a little farther on, although in the completely opposite direction, there's a yogurt parlor that specializes in growing its own bacteria. They make a fine vanilla shake with just a touch of fresh mint. *Something something . . .* if you're in the mood for more substantial nourishment, there are various nearby hamburger stands, sausage stands, and pizza shops—even a Thai restaurant . . . *something something something . . .* fish sauce. All of these are real good eating and they won't break your wallet. But don't worry about that part, honey, because I'm buying. You said your name was what?"

The space between my brain and mouth grew smaller, though still formidable. Into that space Uleene quickly inserted: "I bet you heard plenty of people call Cleveland the 'City of Friendly People.'"

At last, words, like rats running a difficult maze in an unfamiliar laboratory, made their way to my lips. "Actually, I *hadn't* heard that," I said. "Though I'm not surprised. I've only been here a short while, but already I've noticed how many of Cleveland's inhabitants seem to make it their business to make strangers feel happy and comfortable in every way they can, even those individuals who might appear at first outlandish or crude."

I blushed, because I hadn't meant for her to take my comment personally. "I don't mean you, of course. My name is Theodore Bellefontaine. Are you a nurse by any chance?"

Uleene gave her shoulders a cute shrug the way that Monica, in the biker girls movie, used to do. "No problema, and I'm not. I just happen to have read a lot about drugs at one time or another."

Encouraged, I continued. "Thank you very much. As a matter of fact I *would* like to take you up on your kind offer. You don't by any chance know of a decent Chinese restaurant nearby, do you?"

Uleene thought for a moment. "It's not that I don't know of one, but I'm trying to figure out the best. Did you ever hear about a small town in central China where for centuries they've cured their vegetables, and even meats, the natural way—by leaving them out in the sun for a long time? There's a restaurant that does this, and it's not exactly walking distance, but then you weren't doing so well in that department anyway, so if you're up for a little trip on the back of El Diablo, I can have us there in a jiff."

I must have looked puzzled because she added, "Don't be upset, hon. 'El Diablo' is what I call my motorcycle." She pointed to a Harley-Davidson decorated in a Dia de los Muertes motif resting quietly in the shade of a nearby maple tree.

The pigeon had finished off the gum and was pecking on a hot dog a few feet away from my other shoe, which must have come off when I fell. I put it back on, after removing the remaining gum from the first one. Uleene shouldered the bust of Athena and then lowered it carefully into one of the motorcycle's fringed black saddlebags. Then I held on tightly to Uleene's muscular waist as El Diablo roared into life and we headed over the broad streets of Cleveland toward the Truthful Chicken and one of the most fateful Chinese meals I had ever eaten.

The Truthful Chicken hid itself in a little shopping mall between a pizza place and a yogurt parlor. We sat in a red vinyl booth, surrounded by walls of grease-smeared mirrors and lights shaped like red lotus blossoms. I let Uleene do the ordering and watched as the surface of our squarish table with slightly rounded edges filled with a No. 3, a No. 12, a No. 8, and eventually, because she said I could still be dizzy from the fall, a No. 17. While we waited for our meal to arrive Uleene filled me in about her past.

She explained that she was the last surviving member of a motorcycle gang called Satan's Samaritans. The "Samaritans," as she referred to them, had been formed one rainy afternoon in the Greater Northeast Ohio Women's Correctional Institution, and for a time had ranged far and wide over the streets and highways of northeastern Ohio in search of anyone who needed aid, whether they were ready to accept it or not. There had been five original members, counting Uleene—Beth, Lucy, Polly, and Cherise. "It was an attempt to turn around a lot of bad karma, and let me tell you," Uleene continued, smiling as if in recollection of some pleasant memory, "you may think beating up some guy and his old lady in a bar on a Saturday night after a few beers is tough. Well, that's kid stuff compared to trying to help some mom change a flat tire on her station wagon with her three kids running around while she's resisting aid. Sometimes, between taking the old tire off and putting the new one on, plus holding back the mom and kids, it would take all five of us."

"This happened more than once?" I asked.

"All the time. You'd be surprised." She shook her head.

According to Uleene, the gang had started out with real momentum but slowly began to dwindle as one member after another found her free time severely diminished by other activities: Beth by a stormy relationship with her parole officer; Lucy's hobby of real-estate speculation quickly led to a broker's license; and Polly's sideline of baking homemade pies took unexpectedly off into a gourmet catering business. Only Cherise had escaped unscathed by boyfriends or a career; she had simply drifted off to join another gang with a similar mission, Christ's Interveners.

"I could see her point," Uleene said. "A name like that one can really lower the level of consumer resistance."

Encouraged by Uleene's openness, over hot tea and extra egg rolls I spoke of my own career distributing garden tools. "Some of them are nearly works of art," I said, though I thought it best to leave out the propensity of the tools to become implements of hideous crimes. Not that I didn't believe Uleene could handle it, if push came to shove.

"Well," I said, after we had finished eating, "thanks for a wonderful meal, and also for aiding me in the first place when I managed to fall and strike my head. It's only a bit sore by now. I think the MSG probably helped."

Uleene just sat there.

There followed a long and uncomfortable silence during which I checked myself in the mirror and then watched as Uleene concentrated on moving her chopsticks into various shapes: first, an X, then an equals sign, a T, an L, and finally the vertical symbol for parallel lines. At last she left chopsticks alone, and when she looked up her large blue eyes were moist with tears.

"Theodore," she said, "do you ever think about how things that happen are meant to happen and all? Do you believe in fate? How about astrology? Well, not astrology exactly, but how about coincidence?"

It seemed like a trick question, actually four of them, but before I got a chance to answer them, she did.

"Well, I do. For example, me happening to be there just at the moment you knocked yourself out on the water fountain, you being hungry for Chinese food, us having this dinner, and now you, needing so much help, because, as a matter of fact, I have to confess that earlier today I was just about ready to shoot myself in the head because it's so hard to help people in this city where everybody's already happy, thinks they are, or, at a minimum, are able to help themselves. Honestly, sugar," she said, "I was about to quit for good until I stood there and watched you tip over while trying to scrape that piece of gum off your shoe. I'd never seen anything like it. I'm thinking you're a Virgo, am I right?"

Suddenly I was alert, though somewhat embarrassed as well. Was the degree of my need, which I thought I had hidden, that visible? Or had it been pasted on by the stars when I was born? How could this near stranger have known?

"I am," I said.

Uleene turned inward for a minute and formed the chopsticks into the shape of a V. She assumed that expression people put on when they are adding up numbers in their heads. Then she continued. "And it's not just that you fell down in the middle of a sidewalk all by yourself and hit your head on a drinking fountain, or that you are so messed up, but there's something else about you, too. Sure, you could stand to get rid of a few pounds, but you also look like a person who's searching for something, something big, if you know what I mean, but just can't seem to find it. You tell me."

"My mother . . ." I began, and for a reason I was unable to understand my lip began to quiver all on its own.

"Here," Uleene held out her cup. "Drink more tea. What is it, honey? You can tell Uleene. I'm a Libra, and that means I'm here to help."

"Oh, nothing," I said, but it was too late. Uleene had caught the scent of a person who badly needed a Samaritan. She reached across the table and held my wrist in her strong grip.

"This could be crazy, Theodore," she said, "but if you'll just allow me to help you with whatever current problem you're having at the moment, then I'll be able to keep the oath I swore together with my pals of Cell Block B as we stood in a circle around the ping-pong table made of poured concrete and lit by a single bare bulb so many years ago in that light-green cinder-block women's correctional institution recreation room. If a person, especially a Libra, can't keep her promises, she might as well not be alive. So come on, honey. You've come upon me at one of my lowest points ever. What do you say you take advantage of the situation? Help me by letting me help you. Help me keep the spirit of Satan's Samaritans alive. How about it?"

Uleene held out one chopstick in front of her and with her other hand laid a second chopstick across it, balanced in the middle to form a miniature scale. She put the chopsticks down, gazed at her arm, and flexed her bicep. "You don't need anyone rubbed out, do you?"

"Thanks," I said, "but rubbed in, is more like it." I looked at the table, still littered with half-full plates, chopsticks, and a pile of soiled napkins. I looked at Uleene looking at me, a small piece of garlic spinach plastered onto one of her teeth. Then I thought some more. I'd been in Cleveland for well over a month without discovering a single clue or sign of my mother. It was time to stop being so proud.

I stared at what was left of the Twice Regarded Beef in its bed of steamed sesame noodles. "Now that you mention it, there *is* something, or maybe I should say *someone*, I'm interested in," I said. Then I described my whole situation, including the postcards I'd gotten telling me to come to Cleveland. "Do you suppose," I asked, "that if I ever get to the point where I have anything specific to go on you could give me a ride here and there on the back of your motorcycle? And maybe in between you could just sort of keep your ears open for information in general? I know it's asking a lot, and you don't have to make up your mind this very minute. You can think it over."

The waiter glided up with the check along with two fortune cookies wrapped in cellophane. Uleene opened hers. "You are considerate," she read, "and enjoy helping others."

I opened my own cookie. Instead of a fortune, there was a crude drawing of what looked to be a lion on four wheels. Some kind of a car, I guessed, or a float for a parade. I'd never gotten a fortune cookie with a drawing before and I could only assume it was a Cleveland tradition. Then I saw, written in tiny letters on the lion's back, the letters *CU*.

"Look at this," I told Uleene. "Have you ever seen a message in a fortune cookie that looked like this?"

"No," she said, "but I have seen that lion thing. You're looking at the symbol for The Rotary Lions Club, one of the most common sights in this entire city. Originally there used to be two clubs, one Rotary and one Lions, until a few years ago when they both fell on hard times and had to merge. It wasn't easy, though—talk about personalities. That's their new logo."

"But what about those letters?"

"*CU*? That's no mystery at all. See You. It looks to me, sugar, like somebody or someone's trying to get your attention."

"Mother," I managed to gasp.

Uleene studied me. "But I don't get it. If it *is* your mom, then why doesn't she just tell you what's on her mind? Why doesn't she leave a phone number instead of this ridiculous *CU* stuff? Why is she making you go through all of this? What's going on here, anyway?"

"I only wish I knew," I said.

Uleene picked up the bill and reached into the saddlebag that she had carried into the restaurant for what I guessed was her wallet. All at once a different waiter than the one who had originally served us our meal was by our table. We were the only customers left in the place.

"What happened to the waiter we gave our order to?" I asked.

"Oh him," the new waiter answered. "He go home to family. It late."

"And your mom?" Uleene continued to feel around inside the saddlebag.

"I have no idea at all what she's doing at this moment," I said, "but I'm assuming she's dead, if that's what you want to know." I explained about the obituary and all. "But even when she was alive, we never were that close. It's just that I'm worried that somehow, in some way I can't begin to guess, she's in real trouble, maybe for the first time in her life. Why do you think that Rotary Lions symbol—if that's what it's supposed to be—was stuck in my fortune cookie? Do you think our original waiter inserted the note in my fortune cookie and then left, pretending he had a family crisis? If so, why would he do that, unless he didn't want to be questioned about his actions? Do you think someone put him up to it?"

"Ah," Uleene said. "Honey, I should tell you that this isn't the exact symbol for the Rotary Lions, which is actually a much bigger club and dominated entirely by old guys in suspenders. The symbol you're holding is the one for the ladies auxiliary, though it's still one of the largest clubs in Cleveland, bigger even than the Kiwanis. Wait a minute; I've got an idea. You don't happen to have a picture of your mother with you, do you, sugar?"

I did. While I opened my wallet, Uleene went through her saddlebag, taking out various scraps of paper, eyebrow pencils, spark plug wrenches, and several bottles of medication she said was for her back. "Riding cycles is no bed of roses, Theodore, let me tell you."

"I'm really sorry," she added. "It turns out I'm a little short of cash right now. One of the dumb things about me is that I keep offering to buy people dinner, being a Samaritan and all, without first checking to see if I have enough money to pay for it. As long as your wallet is out, would you mind taking care of the bill? I feel real bad, Theodore, but I'll pay you back."

The bill turned out to be surprisingly reasonable. As I waited for my change, Uleene studied the picture of my mother. It had been taken about a week before she had left me in the care of Linda. In it, my mother sat at a table that was piled high with fish, mostly smallmouth bass and what looked like sheepshead. Around her were several burly men holding long-handled nets and cans of beer. In my mother's hand was a fishing rod, and she was wearing a green fishing vest and pearls—a touch I'd always liked. When she was living in St. Nils we had always meant to take an up-to-date picture of just the two of us, but never seemed to get around to it. Then of course, she was gone. Uleene stared at the snapshot a while as if committing it to memory. She returned it to me.

"I'm thinking," she said. She began to stack the cartons of leftover food inside her saddlebag. "Waste not, want not."

"My mother's name is Helen, by the way," I told her. "I know it's an old picture, but she really hasn't changed much. If she's still alive, she'll be in her sixties, a young senior, I think you'd say."

I looked for what must have been the thousandth time at the photo. Back when it was taken had my mother been even then planning to leave me with Linda? Had she already made the trade in her mind: me for more tabletops stacked with more dead fish and yet more cans of beer plus an undetermined amount of cash? Or had my mother paid Linda to take me? I wasn't sure which scenario I preferred.

Uleene sat across from me, her mouth slightly ajar, her skin still flushed from her order of Szechwan beef, momentarily frozen in her outfit of canine tattoo, orange hair, faint scent of motor oil, and motorcycle "colors," as she had told me they were called. I wondered where her own mother was at that moment. Was she dead, alive, or somewhere in between? Was Uleene's mother proud of her?

The piece of spinach had disappeared from Uleene's tooth, and she held the picture up to get a better look. "You two don't look so much alike," she said skeptically, "but for the purpose of your quest, I'm guessing you may as well assume she's still alive. It so happens that there's a meeting of the Women's Rotary Lions coming up tomorrow at noon, and if your mom's alive she may well be there. Somebody might have sent you this clue for a reason, so if you'd like, I can escort you. You'll be my guest, and it will even things out for buying this meal."

The replacement waiter returned with my change. "Thank you so much. I'd like that," I said.

Uleene drove me back to my apartment, and I slept. Toward morning, possibly stimulated by the picture I had showed Uleene, I found myself dreaming of a lake, not one of the Great ones, not Superior or Michigan, or even Erie, on the lower edge of whose eyelid the city of Cleveland rested like a glorious inflammation. No, the one I dreamed of was a smaller, unnamed body of water, one not so overwhelming that a person could get completely lost on it. In this nocturnally emitted body of water were trout, both large-

and smallmouth bass, crappies, and even a few catfish and suckers. In my dream I stood on the shore and called my mother's name above the cries of shore birds and over the splashes of leaping fish.

"Mother, do you hear me? Helen Bellefontaine, are you listening?" I called into the darkness of my dream lake. Nothing answered.

"Helen," I called again. "It's me, Theodore. Your son, remember?"

Still nothing, and so I stood in silence until from far across the lake I could hear the faint putt-putting of an outboard motor. Someone, whether a man or a woman I could not tell, was coming back to shore from a fishing trip. Then the putting became louder until it turned into the sound of a motorcycle's engine revving loudly beneath the window of my apartment.

GUEST: So, Walter, you can imagine my surprise when as clear as anything, I could hear, from practically out of nowhere, an adult voice with what seemed to be a British accent say the word *fossa*. And, I might add, out of all the thousands of words in every language known to man that might be my introduction to eternity, imagine how I felt hearing that one. And would you like to know something even more peculiar? At that exact moment I somehow knew immediately that the "fossa" being referred to was *not* the animal from Madagascar, which, as any school-child can tell you, is half dog and half cat and eats lemurs, but I knew—and please don't ask me how—that the word was actually being used in the precise scientific sense of the word, to indicate the sort of groove, or others might call it a depression, in a bone or in a bird's beak, in other words, that line that runs down the length of the beak to what I believe are called the "nares."

INTERVIEWER: Are those the same things as nostrils? Am I thinking of the same thing?

GUEST: You are, and they are similar, but you are not alone in your confusion, which brings me to the truly interesting part. And that is the fact that for every ten or maybe twenty people who can identify the nares, there's only one who will be able to pick out the word *fossa*, and use it correctly. And then, out of every ten or twenty who get that right, there's maybe only one—two at the most—who can tell you anything at all about the actual posterior fossa, that section of the brain where tumors are among the most problematic, the symptoms of which include headache, neck pain (particularly in the mornings or after a nap), vomiting (especially projectile vomiting, also mornings), blurred vision, dizziness, and swelling. In other words, there I was, Walter, an ordinary certified public accountant, not a specialist in any sense of the word although of course I try to read magazines and newspapers to keep abreast of what is happening, but what I am saying is I am a person without any special scientific or medical training, and suddenly I'm hearing the word *fossa*, and using it correctly, and knowing things I'd never known before.

INTERVIEWER: And the voice was?

GUEST: It was deep, Walter. Really manly, if you know what I mean—like some chief surgeon who's on a medical series on television, or the voiceover on a nature program, and not just any nature program, but one about something that's serious, about extinction, or possibly life after extinction. Maybe on the BBC.

INTERVIEWER: And so what did that tell you about the nature of the afterlife, or the eternal, or whatever you choose to call it?

GUEST: Well, that's exactly the wonderful message I am here to convey. One day you and your listeners may wake up with a slight headache, maybe some projectile vomiting along with it, but it's OK. Here's some free advice: Don't panic. Remember things are simple. Tell yourself that sooner or later everything you need to know about will be taken care of. Not to worry. Relax. Because when the time comes there's going to be a voice, or in some cases people may even get a letter, possibly an e-mail, and while it may not have in it what you want it to have, in any case it will be something that someone somewhere thinks you need to know. In my case, for example, it was *fossa*, but it could be anything. And when it comes you had better be ready. I'm not kidding, Walter.

6

ULEENE HAD CHANGED
into a light-pink voile dress with a scooped schoolgirl collar for the club meeting, but had kept her black motorcycle boots.

"This should be a piece of cake, babe. If your momma's anywhere, she'll be at the Rotary Lions. Are you ready? I came early because I figure you'll probably have your hands full the rest of the day with the tearful reunion, and I thought I might take you out beforehand to a late breakfast. You don't want to go through such a powerful emotional experience as you are about to experience on an empty stomach, do you? What do you say, Mister Dutiful-Son-Soon-to-Be-Reunited-with-His-Long-Lost-Mother?"

Uleene looked great, and the voile somehow accented the muscles of her arms. "Breakfast sounds perfect," I said. "Do you want to surprise me with a place? It's hard for me to think about food right now, although I'm certain that once I sit down I'll have something."

And it was true. I'd heard it said that if not for the city of New Orleans, with its chicory-roasted coffee, plates of sausage, and beignets, and also for San Francisco, with its hot croissants, organic fruit jam, and fresh-ground coffee, and possibly New York, with its hot bialys and bowls of steamed prunes, Cleveland would have been considered the "City of Breakfasts." Accordingly, I was not disappointed by the Muffin Pit, by my two eggs, over easy with a side of bacon, or by my couple pieces of wheat toast and two of those puffy donuts on the side, all prepared by a balding, unshaven, foreign-looking, yet somehow curiously at-home counterman in a grease-spattered white apron. Our orders were delivered, along with a handsome square container of grape preserves, two glasses of orange juice, and two cups of coffee, by a grandmotherly waitress wearing a yellowed doily crown atop her stringy gray hair. I had been keyed up for the meeting, but, needless to say, I suddenly found my appetite.

For her part, Uleene ordered a short stack of buckwheat pancakes, sausage, and a banana. Over coffee she explained that the two clubs had merged back during a time when fitness centers and Internet cafés seemed to be taking over the city's social life. These parvenus had not succeeded, of course, but in those troubled days the Lions Club and the Rotary Club, long rivals, along with their respective auxiliaries, were forced to make peace and combine their memberships in order to survive. Once again, the "can do" nature of Cleveland's population—its ability to take a bad situation and transform it—impressed me.

Uleene peered over her coffee cup. "Actually, they're not completely out of the woods yet, financial-wise," she continued. "They've had to make certain adjustments, but if for some reason your mom's not there, I'm pretty sure at least we'll get a decent meal. Just remember: keep your ears open; you could hear some information that might help you in your search." She squeezed my knee. "I'm afraid I was so worried about dressing and getting to your place in time that I left my money behind in my motorcycle outfit. Do you mind getting this one? Let's lock and load." I paid, leaving a sort of good-luck tip for the waitress, and we walked out into the morning air.

Outside the Muffin Pit, we mounted El Diablo, and all possibility of further conversation was drowned out by the roar of the mighty motorcycle's engine as we passed, as if in a dream, or perhaps in a trailer for a foreign film made entirely of extras, men, women, children, a pack of wild dogs joyously turning a corner in pursuit of a child on a bicycle, a raccoon, a mailman, a robin, and a red squirrel, too—a regular diorama of Cleveland sights and sounds.

Soon we pulled up to the club's headquarters on a by-then wheezing El Diablo ("Bad gas," Uleene had shouted over her shoulder), and I could understand exactly what she had meant when she told me about the club's comedown from its glory days.

Located in one of Cleveland's rare "opportunity zones," the building we parked in front of was not the porticoed mansion that I had more or less imagined, complete with white columns in the Southern style, a garden in back with bright flowers and flowered lounge chairs where weary members could sip hot tea in dainty cups. Instead, the club's headquarters was a windowless version of those potato-shaped donuts formed out of corrugated metal and spray-painted a dull gray. Not only that, but painted on the building's front was the very emblem I had been introduced to at the Truthful Chicken, a lion (gold) on four wheels (red) atop a field of blue, and far from proclaiming the excellence of the organization, it seemed to skulk behind a bed of rag-weed, as if preparing to seize the leg of any passerby who ventured too close. Next door was an auto-body shop.

Uleene knocked the secret knock (one loud, one soft, one loud). "Ted, relax," she told me. "Everything will be fine. I'll be sitting right next to you the whole time." And at first, it did appear that things were going to go as planned. The dowager who was minding the door *did* know and even welcomed Uleene and, because I was with her, me as well. "Who's your boyfriend?" the woman asked her.

"I'm looking for my mother," I said. The lady nodded and, with a grin that looked a lot like the residue of a stroke, pointed wordlessly to the main hall.

And maybe it was to try to lessen the claustrophobic effect of there being no windows, or possibly to make it cheerful (the room *did* have a slightly oppressive feel despite its size), that someone long ago had painted its ceiling a sky blue and the walls on all sides white. But while the intent may have been to make it seem as if we were outdoors—a winter's day in Cleveland with a warming trend—the actual result was more nearly like the aftermath of the sort of accident on an ocean liner that one often reads about: where a gigantic wave has overturned the ship and several passengers find themselves trapped beneath the swimming pool—its bottom having become the ceiling—with the limited oxygen running out and one of them, usually an aging former Olympic swimmer, forced to swim for help.

In the space before me I could see that the small islands of tables surrounded by folding chairs were only half full, as if some of the passengers for this particular cruise had gotten a copy of the weather report and opted out. I took a seat roughly in the center of the room, where I could keep an eye on things, and Uleene sat beside me. At the front of the room, behind the lone lectern, hung the club's banner. Painted on a pale yellow canvas, it was more or less a duplicate of the menacing figure of the wheeled lion outside, but now rampant, an unfortunate choice because it made it look as if the lion were riding a bicycle, or rather a unicycle, in some impoverished rural circus.

Off to one side of the stage was an actual lion, stuffed, with four spoked wheels where its paws should be. I shuddered, imagining someone having had to saw the paws off before attaching the wheels. Including the wheels the lion was about three, maybe four feet tall, and around one of its front legs somebody had looped a piece of plastic clothesline, evidently for pulling it on and off stage. Whether deliberately or accidentally I couldn't tell, a garland of faded crêpe-paper flowers had been draped over the lion's neck. The wheels had been taken from a mountain bike with knobby tires.

Despite Uleene, I was starting to feel uncomfortable. I was the only man present; my mother was nowhere to be seen. What if she did appear? Would it be from the dead, wearing the trappings of the tomb, leaving behind a trail of pond water like some actress in a low-budget horror flick? No, I told myself. That would be just plain silly.

While I waited for the meeting to officially start I took out the picture of my mother and passed it among several ladies near our table. While two of the women present claimed to have seen her, I had the distinct impression it was only because they did not want any son to be disappointed. "You are such a good boy to be doing this. If only my own son, who is an orthodontist, cared as much about his mother as you do," a gray-haired matron said, and I felt a blush of mixed pleasure and shame at having done so little. I had my excuses, naturally, but this certainly wasn't the audience to hear a critique of motherhood.

All at once I found myself being called to attention by a large lady wearing a light-blue safari hat with a long veil hanging down the back, the kind of hat women used to wear in old adventure movies.

"Excuse me," she said, "honored members and"—she looked at me—"guest. Today we are fortunate to have as our special speaker Doorperson Muriel Collins, who has come to share with us her thoughts on life and death, a subject I am sure we all will find of interest."

Uleene reached over to give my shoulder a little rub. "Be patient, honey," she whispered. "There's still a chance your mother might show up, and if not, there's the food." It wasn't reassuring; and, anyway, after that late breakfast

I wasn't very hungry. I scanned the audience to see if I could identify which one of the twenty or so women present might be Doorperson Muriel. I guessed she might be the woman near the front who was wearing a white robe—a choir robe, it looked like—and a turban made of shiny silver material. Oddly, the ladies around me seemed not at all nonplused by this strange outfit. Was this the designated garb for all who would come to address these lady Rotary Lions, some mandatory outfit to set them apart? Then the woman walked boldly to the lectern, and her first words answered my question.

"Greetings, members of this esteemed organization," she began. "Today in order to emphasize the importance of my message to you, I come clad in the official dress uniform of my own more ancient group, the Fellowship of the Open Door, even though you may be sure our normal daily garb is more practical and less attention-grabbing."

I thought I could detect a measure of condescension in her voice, but despite her slightly officious tone, Doorperson Muriel, a mild-looking woman in her midthirties, lightened the effect of her announcement with an ingenuous smile.

"Now, because time is limited, I'd like to get to the heart of my message first and then explain it afterward, so if you don't mind, here goes: Namely, it is that the hereafter is not at all what you may think. Neither, for that matter, is the past, nor the here and now."

Finally we were getting somewhere. Clearly this mild Doorperson, or whatever she called herself, was no pushover, but in fact embraced a tougher philosophy than many so-called men. The subject of the hereafter seemed to be on the right track, too. Again I looked around the room for my mother but didn't see her. *Well of course*, I thought, *my mother is dead*. What had I been thinking?

But in that case, *why* had I come to Cleveland?

To my surprise, however, the women in the audience, perhaps through the wisdom that is supposed to arrive with mounting years, looked unimpressed by Doorperson Muriel's revelation. In fact they seemed almost blasé. Had they heard this speech before, or was this sort of information common knowledge here in the Midwest? Alternately, was Doorperson Muriel no more than a fixture on the Cleveland women's club circuit—a known commodity who could be counted on to provide a good afternoon's entertainment without embarrassing any of its members? And if so, was she the kind of person who left one feeling vaguely pleased with one's own life, either because one hadn't gone so far as to join a cult like this poor woman had, or because a person realized that whatever Muriel was saying, her listeners had known it all along? I looked at Uleene. She was using her teeth to rip apart the wrapper on a package of crackers with sesame seed sprinkles.

Doorperson Muriel started to hum, of all things, and I felt the hairs on the backs of my arms rise. Serving people passed among us handing out cups of canned fruit cocktail with sprigs of fresh mint. Uleene looked at me with an "I told you so" expression.

As the servers drew closer to our table, Doorperson Muriel pulled herself up a little straighter and looked down at those of us who were sitting on our uncomfortable metal folding chairs. "You may be enjoying your fruit cocktail at this moment," she seemed to hum, "but that pleasure will pale in comparison to what you will learn if you begin to take the long view, as have the members of the Fellowship of the Open Door."

Her lips parted.

I waited.

Her lips parted wider and the humming grew louder. It felt as if my ears were starting to ring. Then she paused. She seemed distracted by something happening in the back of the room. Clearly, she was deciding whether we were ready to receive her message. Then, just as she appeared to decide that we were, but before any actual words could actually make their way to us, from behind me I heard the sounds of a scuffle.

I turned, hopeful that I would see my mother, and for a moment I imagined her connecting with a roundhouse on some bossy club member who had tried to keep her from reuniting with her son, but I was disappointed. Where Mother should have been was only an ancient, narrow woman with a great shock of bluish-white hair, now completely undone, tugging on a folding chair, the other end of which was being grasped by a sturdy, roundish woman in a flowered smock, her stubbly hair short enough to be the result of a dose of chemo or radiation treatments.

"Uh-uh," Uleene said. "There they go again." She quickly explained that the two women had been the former presidents of the Lions and the Rotary before the clubs joined forces, and each suspected her husband of having a fling with the other. "Also," she added, "they've never really gotten over losing control of their own organizations. Those old rivalries die hard."

But whatever medical procedures these ladies may have undergone in the past, that day they were surprisingly fit. Though the chair was yanked back and forth, neither would let go. Suddenly, the Lioness feinted to the left and, as the Rotarian leaned to follow, stuck out her foot, toppling her rival to the floor. Once on the floor, however, the Rotarian's relatively compact form worked in her favor. Releasing her hold on the chair and bending her arms to protect her head, she rolled furiously into the Lioness, hitting her squarely in her knees, bringing both her and the chair she was triumphantly clutching down with a crash. Then, abandoning all pretext of the chair—because there had been plenty of vacant chairs all along—from the floor the Lioness let loose a stinging jab that opened a nasty cut over the Rotarian's left eye, possibly caused by the frame of her pearl-colored eyeglasses being pushed into her occipital cavity. Undeterred, the Rotarian, blood streaming down her cheek, got the Lioness into a powerful headlock and squeezed hard.

"Shirley, help me out on this," the Lioness roared, and a svelte woman in designer jeans sailed across a row of seats in a kind of septuagenarian karate leap. Seeing this, other women, presumably former Lions and ex-Rotarians, came forth to help their respective leaders. I couldn't help but notice how fit the elders of Cleveland seemed to be.

Uleene grabbed my arm and picked up her motorcycle bag from beneath the chair where it had been resting. "That's it," she said. "We're getting out of here." She waded through the crowd, swinging her bag, which looked as if it had been packed for just this sort of situation with several rolls of nickels.

I took a couple minor hits, plus one nasty blow to the side of my head, in part because I'd never been much of a fighter, but also because it was hard to bring myself to strike someone even older than my mother. Uleene, however, who must have learned to defend herself during her prison years, had no such compunction, and she rapidly cleared a path for us. By the time we reached the door the place was a mess: I could see a couple of the more frail ladies lying gasping on their sides and one was looking pretty gray, as if her heart or some other serious organ might have failed. I looked around one last time for my mother. She wasn't there.

"And they put *me* in the slammer," Uleene told me as we walked toward El Diablo. "Those old ladies should be ashamed of themselves. I feel bad for you, sugar, but don't worry. This town's loaded with women's clubs. I only wish we had some new clue as to where to look next. I would have bet money that this Rotary Lions thing would pan out."

I climbed onto the back of El Diablo after removing a small plastic trident, such as one might find in a cocktail glass stuck into an olive or a cherry. Someone had inserted it beneath the leather strap across the backseat. It certainly had not been there on my earlier ride. It wasn't dangerous in the least, of course, and I thought it was probably the whimsical offering of some drunken passerby.

I waved it in front of Uleene's face to show her my souvenir, and she said something back, but with the wind and all, I couldn't understand a word.

spoke by phone to Marty, who seemed to be doing wonders with the gardening implement business.

"Things are fabulous here, better and better," Marty would say each time I called. Apparently, since criminals had made my line of implements their tools of choice, sales had been heading skyward. Each week I would check my balance in the bank; Marty was telling the truth. Several times I offered to fly back, but he assured me there was no need. "Don't be silly; enjoy yourself," he said. "Look around—gosh, Cleveland! Who *wouldn't* want to be *there*?"

I wasn't a native, of course, but I *was* beginning to feel at home. It seemed like a good idea to use some of the time I had left over from art classes and such to explore the city out to its suburbs and beyond. Maybe if I broadened my net, I might be more successful. With that in mind, I took a whole day to visit the souvenir and card shops in all the Heights: Shaker, Garfield, Maple, Cleveland, University, Broadview, and Richmond, though without any luck. Shortly after that I took another day and trudged to the Villes: Strongsville, Warrensville, Brecksville, and the most tantalizing of all, Remindersville, from which location I looked back at where I'd just been. And what *had* Remindersville reminded me of? Absolutely nothing at the time, but later that evening, when I returned to my apartment and, over a simple supper of raised donuts and fried potatoes, studied the map of where I'd traveled that day, I *was* reminded that I had failed to see a famous scenic spot not far from Remindersville, a spot known far and wide not only for its beauty but also as a productive fishing hole in its own right, the very spot I had been avoiding ever since my arrival. It was, of course, the site of my mother's "death," the last landscape she had seen before its waters had closed over her—Aurora Pond. Alone in my room, chewing silently on a one of those donuts, I vowed I would go there first thing next morning.

Named after the goddess of the dawn, Aurora Pond was in the suburbs to the east and south of the bustling city. Having gotten a bit of a late start—I slept past the first two buses—I arrived there closer to noon than to the break of day as I'd intended. Leaving the bus, I walked through the gate and up the driveway to the pond itself, and absorbed the shimmer of its quiet beauty through shy cattails and the stubborn mudflats that hosted all manner of fishermen in various stages of embarking and disembarking, untangling their lures from branches and slimy roots, urinating, or just stopping to eat a leisurely lunch, leaving behind only sandwich wrappers, Styrofoam carryout cartons, and crushed beer cans as silent, fumbling offerings to the goddess of the dawn, herself having passed her expiration hour. Far from the sinister cesspool I had feared, all I saw was a calm and soothing mirror to the sky. It was easy to see why my mother had come here to find peace. Why, I asked myself, had I waited so long?

Here and there along those parts of the pond's edges that were inaccessible to fishermen I could see carcasses of beached fish that, having managed to dislodge an imperfectly presented lure or cough up a ball of cheese with (surprise!) a treble hook inside, had nonetheless succumbed to their wounds, so even as they had outwitted Death's barbed minions, they had failed to outswim the Swimming Master himself. Over and among their white-bellied bodies crows walked, pecking experimentally and cawing here and there.

Also here and there were dragonflies, harbingers, in their insect way, of the swarms of giant fish bats that—as a descriptive brochure I had found lying on the ground by my feet explained—appeared at dusk each evening to prey on the younger catfish, perch, bass, and sheepshead all stocked by the pond's manager, because, according to the same brochure: "Second only to the pleasure of the fishermen who arrive here from all corners of the world is our pledge to maintain the delicate ecological balance of this sacred environmental showplace. We gather not only to fish," the brochure's unintendedly prophetic words explained, "but also to watch how Death greets Life on a daily basis."

How true that was for Helen Bellefontaine, I could not help but think.

The author of this brochure, who happened also to be the pond's manager, was someone named "Sarge," and the name, though common enough, reminded me (Oh Remindersville, indeed!) of something I couldn't quite put my finger on at that moment. I thought just possibly that Linda might have mentioned that name once or twice back in St. Nils, but it would have been years ago, when I was a child, and whether it was that or the name was simply that of a colorful character out of a television show from my youth I could not be sure.

The bats and night birds, however, and even the mysterious "Sarge," were for later. Right then, at high noon, I watched the lazy rowboats dotting the surface of the lake like elongated fungi, each moored to some "favorite spot" by a gallon paint can full of hardened concrete attached to a plastic rope that in turn was tied to a ring at the front of each numbered boat, allowing it to pivot like a single hand of a clock, some registering minutes, others slowly circling the hours, while others were in between, running sometimes fast and sometimes slow depending on the wind and currents.

I stared, hypnotized by the pond's calm surface. The water, a coffee-with-not-enough-cream color, was as motionless as a tabletop in an actual coffee shop (where else?), the kind of place decorated in deep browns and crimsons, tints no doubt meant to evoke a feeling of smoldering richness and well-being, as opposed to the garish reds and oranges of fast-food joints, which, I supposed, were meant to evoke the sudden wildfires of appetite as well as to induce a certain desperation to put out the flames. But that day at least, the pond was pristine except for a few gum wrappers and wind-driven empty Styrofoam worm containers that blew like miniature ghost ships across a surface that looked almost solid enough to walk on, not at all the sort of place where anyone, let alone a person's mother, could be sucked under to drown.

I waved away a largish fly.

Off in the distance, to my right, was Sarge's Bait, a picturesque shack that I knew must contain a seemingly endless supply of hellgrammites, crickets, night crawlers, red worms, cheese balls, salmon eggs, and desperate minnows doomed to a sort of living death as they waited, only too unaware that their present cramped quarters were fated to be the very glory days of their existence. For how could these small, earnest-looking fish know that what would follow would only be a choice of being hooked through the lips (swimming in a more or less natural fashion, with a chance of about one in fifty of the lips tearing away from the hook from the force of the cast to send it flying to freedom), being hooked through the body below the spine, the fisherman careful to miss the spine itself (a more natural swim but an early death, as one would imagine, and zero chance of survival), or being hooked through the tail (superior for attachment, but resulting in a completely weird and unnatural swimming motion once it hit the water, the odds for survival unknown)?

Unlike most ordinary bait shacks, however, with their square cinder-block construction and tasteless paint jobs, Sarge's Bait was in its way a triumph of form and content, blending into the ecosystem of the lake's pristine waters thanks to a combination of weathered wood, overgrown vines, and generally shoddy workmanship. On one side, a part of and yet separate from the bait shack, was a back porch, a smaller structure called Sarge's Boat Rentals by the Day. From it dribbled out a narrow path that led down to a small dock and then to the pond.

I continued to stare from afar at the two buildings, so like a mother and child (or so it seemed to me) in this near wilderness. In front of the boat-rental place, like yet another child (this one in a stroller), I spotted a man—I presumed it was Sarge himself. He was seated in an aluminum lawn chair. He wore a sleeveless shirt and a military cap. He sipped a Diet Sprite. I was a little far away at that point to jump to conclusions, but it was hard not to believe that here was a man who would not have been out of place if he had been somehow instantly lifted out of this bucolic setting and dumped upon an ice floe, for example, somewhere in the distant Arctic, staring as thoughtfully and silently as a king walrus, alert for enemies. But for that matter, neither was Sarge out of place at Aurora Pond. Although at that very minute his eyes were shut, as a man of nature he was undoubtedly listening for the slightest signs of trouble from the boats still out on the lake to be sure that none of them was about to be hijacked into the back of a waiting pickup truck by some lowlife who'd laid down a false ID.

I was of two minds: wary, but fascinated.

Was it possible that this same Sarge—unshaved, brutish, and considerably gone to seed—was, in the actual words of the pond's brochure, also "a man of considerable scientific acumen and environmental consciousness, part sportsman, part naturalist, part entrepreneur, and part law-of-nature's enforcement officer"? The concept boggled my mind, as did the thought that it was this exact Sarge, currently draped over a cheap lawn chair and holding a beverage, who must have been the very person to find my mother floating facedown (or up), lodged in a clump of weeds or bumping up against a muddy bank on that tragic day not so long ago. I shivered despite the warmth of the afternoon. Should I walk up to the man and ask him for details? I knew I should, but what would he say? Would he describe to me how she had looked that day, wet and possibly swollen and covered with flies? Would he describe how they dragged my mother to shore and put her dripping into the back of a coroner's van? I didn't think I could bear that part.

"You can wait a while," I said.

"No, you can't," I answered.

I shut my eyes and breathed and listened. The lake was quiet, except for the occasional slap of an oar on the water, the zing of a spinning reel, and some mumbled curse as a lunker got away or a line became entangled in a water plant or anchor rope. I opened my eyes. I didn't seem to be moving either toward Sarge or away.

"You have come all this way, Theodore," I mumbled to myself. "You *must* finish what you started." I got up from the hillock where I'd been having this argument with myself and began to walk toward the reclining pond manager. Cautiously, like a fisherman sneaking up to the edge of a bank in whose shadows a giant trout rests, I approached the dozing supervisor of nature. His eyes, unlike a fish's, remained shut. Could I be sure what he would do when I approached him? I could not.

At last I stood about ten feet from the lounge chair in which the man reclined. On one of his massive forearms was a tattoo of a bowling ball with wings and on the other was a trout, much like the one I had metaphorically evoked moments earlier, but this dermatically engraved specimen had a royal coachman fly caught in his upper lip and was leaping out of a still pool. I caught a strong scent of body odor mixed with sunscreen.

"Ahem," I said.

There was no reaction. Could it be that *he* was dead as well? It was a strange thought, but not, after all, very likely.

I cleared my throat again and suddenly, like the very tattooed trout on his right forearm, the man bolted up and shot from his chair. He had a wild look in his eyes.

"Excuse me," I said, but before I could introduce myself properly, Sarge (if indeed it was Sarge) completely ignored me to run full speed toward the dock, pounding on its wooden members in a thunderous gallop. Next he leapt into an attractively painted red and black motorboat, pulled the starter, was immediately enveloped in a cloud of blue smoke until, flicking some lever or another, he finally raced off across the lake, leaving only the smoke behind.

Had he sensed something that I, with my city-trained eyes had missed? Had he detected some danger to the wild-life living under his protection? Did he have a telephone implanted in the ear on the opposite side of his head from where I was standing and through it received a call from some boater in distress? I never found out. All I knew is that one minute he was there, apparently snoozing, and the next he was somewhere out on the surface of Aurora Pond, on a mission. I waited by the dock as boatload after boatload of tired but happy fishermen disembarked with heavy string-ers of bass, catfish, trout, and bluegill, tied up their boats, and left, but Sarge, or at least the person I assumed to be Sarge, never returned.

Finally, I took the last bus back to the city, and by the time I arrived at my apartment it was nearly dark. There were a few punters still capsizing out on the river, and over-head a police helicopter appeared to be searching for some-one. I was about to walk upstairs, turn the lights on, and run a hot bath when I saw Raul in the window of Love Hurts, waving at me to come inside. He looked agitated, and once across from him I could hear he was breathing rapidly. Raul wasn't a bad guy, and though I didn't know him as well as I had Ramon, I'd grown to respect him during my time above Love Hurts. We often exchanged pleasantries, and I used to nod whenever I passed the window and saw him standing behind the counter.

"Ted," he said, "you've got to help me—I'm desperate. Janice is having her baby way ahead of schedule, and I still have two hours to go before the end of my shift. You don't by any chance know how to work a cash register, do you?"

I looked at the register used by Love Hurts. It was of the old-fashioned variety, and as luck would have it the exact same model I had worked at a pet shop where I had been employed one summer as a boy. I nodded.

"Can you please take over? You know how nervous Janice gets. If I get there in time I promise I'll name the baby after you."

I had met Janice. She was a tall, thin girl with dark, straight hair, very pale skin, and dark rings under her eyes. When I'd first arrived at Love Hurts and Janice was in the emotional stages of her pregnancy she would come to sit at the counter with Raul and weep until the boss forbade her. He claimed she drove away business, but speaking for myself, I thought she brought a woman's touch to the store.

"Sure," I told Raul. "You take care of Janice and don't worry about me. I'll be fine."

So I worked the register for the next two hours, at first throwing in a friendly nod with every purchase, but I soon found out that in the world of saucy photos and sexual-stimulation devices the last thing anyone wanted was real human contact. After I told an old guy that I hoped his purchases would give him the satisfaction he craved, he actually turned around and carefully put everything in his shopping basket back on the shelves. On his way out he paused to shake his head reproachfully. "Nosey Parker," he said. After that I just took their money, swiped their credit cards, and stuck whatever they'd bought in the store's plain brown-paper bags. Clearly, this was an entirely different world than that of the gardening business, where people were only too happy to hang around for hours chatting about the composition of their soil or the singularities of their growing conditions. Nonetheless, I noted that, while Cleveland had surprisingly few so-called perverts for a town of its size, those who might fit that description were unfailingly good mannered. Even the lady flasher who came in toward the end of my stand-in for Raul, though she was clearly disappointed to find me instead at the register, still took the time to flip open a beautifully tailored fur coat for a heartbeat, and then smiled sweetly on her way out.

When Raul returned, he gave me a cigar with a pink bow. "Thanks, Ted," he said. "Theodora is a beauty, and both Janice and I are grateful."

"Congratulations," I answered. "Be sure to give Janice a big hug for me, won't you?"

"You bet," he said, and took my place behind the counter to finish his shift.

I went upstairs and went straight to bed.

> **tape four**

HOST: And here this afternoon we've brought along with us someone you just might recognize from your past, so to speak.

DAD: Tommy, is that you?

TOMMY: Yes, Dad, it's me, Tommy, your long lost son, and thanks to the wonderful people at *Together Again*, I'm seeing you again for the first time since I was two.

DAD: Oh, Tommy, Tom, and I thought you were . . .

HOST: Say it. Don't hold back.

DAD: Dead. But that sounds so horrible in front of you

now. Still, I'm afraid I have to admit that's what I was thinking.

TOMMY: Don't feel bad. That's almost what I thought, too. After all those years of drugs, and imprisonment, and working as a music reviewer for various obscure magazines, writing those articles about bands that had already split apart by the time the article got published, and writing poetry, too—I wrote an awful lot of poetry that several published poets I read it to said showed real promise— anyway, I thought that by the time I ever got around to finding you if I ever did, you'd be, well . . . you know . . .

HOST: Dead?

TOMMY: No. But really old.

DAD: And now? Now what do you think?

TOMMY: I think I'm really, really glad to see you at least once before you . . .

HOST: Die? You can say it if that's what you really mean, Tommy.

TOMMY: I meant get any older.

DAD: Tommy.

TOMMY: Dad. And so now you can tell me what you were doing all those years we've been apart.

DAD: Well, you know. After I left your mother I went on a sort of spiritual journey: yoga, meditation, getting as centered as possible. In other words, I'm finally becoming one with the universe. I changed my diet and now take nothing but homeopathic medicine. I also spend as much time as I can spare chanting.

HOST: You mean Om? Is that why you are dressed in all those natural fibers?

DAD: Yes, that's it. Om, or, as my teacher, Guru Jee, likes to say, the sound of the universe after a colonic. And, Tommy, it seems to me you've been on a spiritual quest of your own, but of an entirely different kind.

TOMMY: Well, I *am* your son.

DAD: Yes, you certainly are. Om. Shall the two of us try to say it together, right now on this radio program?

TOMMY: You mean Om? Well, sure. Look, I just said it.

DAD: No, I mean to say it together. Om.

HOST: Wait. How about all three of us?

TOMMY: OK. Here goes: Om.

DAD: Om. That wasn't right: again.

ALL: Om.

DAD: Were getting there. Don't give up. Let's try again: one, two, three . . .

ALL: Om.

HOST: And an Om to you, our listeners, from the program that reunites the lost particles with the larger whole, *Together Again*. Good night.

8

the birth of Theodora, the countertop of Love Hurts was awash in baby pictures, which didn't seem to have any dampening effect on business, as far as I could tell, but which did have an impact on me, after a fashion. Looking at all those pictures of the rapidly growing baby, it struck me that I'd been in Cleveland for a couple months by then and, except for Uleene, Raul, and my teacher, Sunshine, I knew practically no one. I took long walks, attended free concerts, and read the *Plain Dealer*, but Cleveland's citizens turned out to be tougher to get to know than they originally had seemed. It got to the point where I would stop complete strangers to show them my mother's picture; they were polite and often sympathetic, but they had their own lives to live, their own children to raise. I understood. The photos of Theodora rested on the counter, her face and body mutating from one week to the next, reminding me that time was passing and yet I was no closer to finding my own mother than when I first arrived. My life was on hold. I had tried to be patient, but what kind of son did that make me? True, I was busy with my art, but the fact was my mother had never expressed much of an interest in art, despite all the years she'd spent in Cleveland. I'd left a couple messages for Uleene but had heard nothing back. And yes, the gardening implement business was running well without me, but I needed a plan. I needed something else to try. I was beginning to feel like a failure.

Then, through a set of circumstances that had nothing at all to do with Uleene, or Raul, or the art world, fate intervened. *The Plain Dealer*, in an effort to increase its shaky circulation, had a policy to let no rat attack on an infant or small child go unreported, so much so that one of my favorite columns appeared every Thursday at the back of the paper next to the crossword puzzle. It was called The Rat Log and described each attack in graphic detail, including pictures, when available. Thus it was no surprise that some citizens had taken to calling their city, affectionately, the "City of Rats." But then, when several rats, one of them the size of a large badger, in broad daylight attacked and actually killed a councilman who had been on his way to give a speech to a group of fourth graders about the dangers of drugs ("City of Pot?" the *Plain Dealer*'s headline had asked just a week earlier), the remaining members of the city council voted, with only one abstention, to declare an entire day, a Saturday, dedicated to beating back the menace of these increasingly bold creatures.

To accomplish this task, the city offered a metal garbage-can lid and also a small wooden club to anyone who wished to participate. Both of them would have to be signed for and returned at the end of the day they were used, however, so they could be properly cleaned. "You don't want to be dealing with dried rat blood," the newspaper quoted someone they identified as "an old-timer" saying. Newcomers and short-term visitors to the city in particular, the article said, were invited to stop by the nearest firehouse and sign up for the event, which the paper compared to the Running of the Bulls in Pamplona.

In Cleveland, however, the paper said, everyone would be a member of a two-person team and as such would have a great chance to make new friends. *Friends*, I thought. I walked around the corner to the closest fire station, signed up, and collected my club and lid. "And who is going to be the other member of my 'combat team?'" I asked a burly hook-and-ladder driver. He wrote down my name and gave me the kind of look that said I must be new to Cleveland. "Relax. You have to be patient," he said in a piece of advice that was starting to sound familiar. "You'll find out soon enough."

When Rat Saturday arrived, I was wakened at 6:00 AM by a knocking on my door. I opened it and was surprised to see a mountain of a woman wearing a well-used army camo jacket with the ends of its sleeves secured at the wrists by rubber bands. From the waist down she wore gray ski pants that were tucked neatly into a pair of scuffed leather combat boots. My new friend turned out to be not new at all, but Sunshine. "I live down the block, and the firemen matched us up," she said. "You can imagine how happy I was to see that my partner for the day was going to be a fellow artist— not that such a thing is all that unusual in this town."

"I guess so," I said. "Where's your husband? Is he coming with us?"

"Naw," she said. "Jim's at home watching nature specials on television. He turned down keeping me company on the rat hunt because he claims he can't stand this cruelty to animals stuff, but my ancestors come from Hungary, one of the many nationalities that call Cleveland their home, and we are among the best rat hunters anywhere." I noticed that Sunshine had with her a plastic lid from what looked to be a kitchen garbage pail and a club made out of an old polo mallet. Into the handle she had carved a sort of frieze depicting a rat hunt somewhere—it looked to be in a jungle. The head of the mallet had been freshly varnished.

"Those government-issued clubs may be OK for amateurs," she said, "but to my people, who have centuries of ratting in our blood, they smack a bit of the amateur. Don't you worry, Ted. I'll stick nearby in case you get into trouble."

While Sunshine explained the advantages of a smaller, lightweight shield, she held out her club so I could feel its heft; it seemed lethal enough. Into one end of the mallet's head was a nail that had been filed to a sharp point.

"Do you really need that?" I asked.

She shook her large head. "Honestly, no," she said. "But to tell the truth, we Hungarians like to see a little gore."

The dawn was just beginning to smear its marmalade glow over the east as Sunshine and I walked down the empty streets, pausing every so often to listen for the sounds of garbage can lids banging in the distance. We paused but, strangely, all we could hear was what sounded like a single lid, and far away, at that.

"Where *is* everyone?" I asked Sunshine. "Do you think we got the day wrong? I thought this was the day we were supposed to all walk forward beating on our trash can lids in order to drive the rats into Progressive Field, the home of the Cleveland Indians baseball team, where we're then supposed to finish the rats off before the doubleheader."

Sunshine gave me a gloomy look. She silently lifted her modified mallet to signal that she had not relaxed her vigilance.

All to no avail.

We walked together for an hour in the thin light of early dawn with Sunshine making various comments of an artistic and sculptural nature along the way, but saw no rats at all. We strode by nightclubs and businesses, newsstands and adult entertainment centers, all shut tight. We had just passed by several dozen overflowing garbage cans when I gave my shield a whack to see if that would strike enough panic into the heart of a rat to force him or her out into the open, but either it was the wrong type of sound to strike fear or the rats had somehow sensed our plan and were lying low.

From out a window somewhere, a guy yelled at me to shut up.

"This stinks," Sunshine said. "It's time for Plan B. I guess our fellow citizens are not so concerned over their own welfare and the health of their elected officials as the *Plain Dealer* wished us to believe."

Just as I was about to inquire what exactly Plan B was, suddenly, from out of an encampment of cans I had given up on, a rat the size of a spaniel hurled itself straight at my throat, using as a springboard a cardboard box that had once held a microwave. Before it could connect, however, Sunshine's superb Hungarian reflexes leapt into action. The polo mallet lashed out with a satisfying thwack and knocked the beast senseless. I stopped to look. It *was* a spaniel, evidently some stray who had been surviving for weeks by rummaging through the neighbors' garbage pails, still with his blue nylon collar and his tag in the shape of a dog bone that read "Buddy."

"What the hell," Sunshine said. "Plan B is as follows: We quit the rat hunt and stop for a beer." She pointed to the Diamond Bar and Grill about a half block ahead of us, which, if I could judge by the rapidly diminishing line in front of it, had just that moment thrown its doors open for business. I told her that it was a little early for me, but that she should go ahead; I'd keep her company with a coffee or something. I was feeling grateful.

The interior of the bar was still mostly a bluish dark, with spots of ochre where the sun had managed to claw its way in through the windows, and I was surprised to see, despite the early hour, a sizable crowd had settled in.

"Yo, Sunny," one of them called. "Who's your boyfriend? Does Jim know about him? How's the art world treating you these days?"

Of course I was embarrassed, as anyone would be, but at the same time somewhat pleased that finally I was meeting new people. I looked at the man who had just spoken. He was a large person with thick gray hair braided into greasy pigtails. He wore a heavy steel chain around his hairy neck.

"My name is Ted," I answered, "and we've been out all morning killing rats."

"Rats," he mused. He introduced himself as Yellow Horse.

"Well, actually, only a stray dog so far," Sunshine answered, "but it's a thirsty business."

By the time Sunshine was ready to leave the Diamond Bar it was about noon, and though I had to admit that she held her beer well, I was starting to get jittery from all that coffee. We were just getting up to go, when Yellow Horse stopped me.

"Ted, wait a minute," he said, and pulled out three match-sticks. He slid them over to me. "You're new to Cleveland, so I'll bet you haven't seen this one. If you can make four out of this, I'll grant you any wish you want. And you can't break any of the matches, either." I caught him winking at Sunshine. He took out another match, struck it, and lit a small, brown, foul-smelling cigar, the same kind that he had been smoking all morning.

I took two of the sticks and made a sideways V, then put the remaining stick against the wide part of the V so its top touched the top matchstick of the V and the other stick of the V rested on its middle. It looked like a pennant, or a four. "How's that?" I said. "There's your four."

"I'll be damned," Yellow Horse said. "So what's your wish?"

And I don't know whether it was the welcoming atmo-sphere of the Diamond Bar and Grill, or the smell of that cigar making me dizzy, or if I was just tired from having gotten up so early that morning only to sit around and watch others drink beer after beer, but I thought I'd give it a try. "Well," I said, "a few months ago, while I was living in a far-away city you've probably never heard of, I got a postcard from my dead mother telling me to come to Cleveland. I'm here doing what she asked, but she's either lost or hiding. I have to say I'm getting really frustrated; I don't suppose there's any way you could help me out, is there?"

Yellow Horse shut his eyes. At that moment he looked more like a swamp turtle than a horse, I thought—a big swamp turtle who had spent the greater part of his life swimming and basking on a log in an ancient lake, or maybe a pond like Aurora Pond, but one filled mostly with lager.

He opened his eyes. "I don't exactly know," he said, "but I'll try. I'll use what I remember of my Native American heritage, even though it's been considerably degraded by the crass commercialism of all these years of living in this so-called civilization the white man has substituted for our native culture." Then he shut his eyes again, really tightly this time.

"I see a hot place, pitchforks, or tridents, or maybe those long forks people use to fish maraschino cherries out of a gin and tonic—I can't really tell. I see fumes, and mist, and fog. The word *devil* comes to mind, but I don't know why, exactly. I hope this is not bad news. Was your mother a good person?" He opened his eyes and finished his beer.

"Actually, I don't know," I said. "Even when she was still alive we weren't all that close. But thanks for your concern. The fact is that your description reminds me a lot of a place

I passed today while Sunshine and I were out pounding the streets for rats. Have you ever heard of the Hot Club?"

Then Yellow Horse went deep to his swamp-turtle self again. He shut his eyes. "Of course," he answered. "Who hasn't?"

9

THE WINDOWLESS front of the Hot Club was bright red, with a painted border of yellow flames that sprang waist-high from the sidewalk, arrested but not extinguished, so it looked as if the building were perpetually in the process of burning down. Above the flames, buoyed by squiggly lines that I supposed were meant to represent hot air rising, someone had drawn bright balloons. On each balloon a phrase such as "Hold Me," "Burning Up," or "Oh Baby" was inscribed. The flame theme continued at the front door as well, with a ring of painted fire surrounding the door's handle. Over the door itself were the words, done in a sort of writhing typography, "Take Hope, All Ye Who Enter Here."

I was greeted at the entrance by an affable woman in a pink terry-cloth robe, and I walked inside to see a stage surrounded by the same red and yellow flame motif as the exterior. Seated beneath the stage, on orange folding chairs around small tables with red tablecloths, were the club's members, entirely women, though at the Hot Club the women were not predominantly the motherly types who had swelled the thin ranks of the Rotary Lions. No, these were more like older sisters, and they appeared in various stages of attractive dishabille, wearing slips and half slips, garter belts, Merry Widows, push-up bras, fishnet stockings, wigs (or hair that had been styled to look like wigs), peignoirs, robes, and kimonos—all the accoutrements of the boudoir—as if these adopted big sisters had only minutes ago rolled out of their beds fresh from a dream of a sexy date and just happened to find themselves here at the Hot Club, where, magically, the innuendo-laden promise of hope engraved above the door might just be able to rub away death, disfigurement, disability, and dismemberment, might be just the ticket to chase away the surgeon's knife, shrink up tumors, lift sagging skin, erase the befuddlement of Alzheimer's, smooth away wrinkles, and destroy once and for all the nightmares of coming old age. The place was pretty crowded and, despite the fact that I was the only male present, no one seemed to take offense at my being there. To the contrary, they seemed pleased. I walked toward a table on one side of the room where I could sit and keep an eye out for my mother.

It was embarrassing, in a way, to be seeing these women caught up in their fantasies of unbridled, youthful passion but, on the other hand, I thought how optimistic of them as well, that these club members—driven, if not to the very brink of the grave, at least to the entrance of the cemetery by the pitiless motor of time—were still game to carpe the diem, to leap, leap, leap again, like a dying salmon into its fifteenth or sixteenth waterfall, and not even necessarily to spawn, because, truth to tell, several of them appeared to be past the age for actual spawning. This thought was interrupted when Mitzie and Carla, a blonde and a redhead respectively, joined me at my table. Mitzie wore a black slip and pearls, while Carla was in a sort of housecoat with a boa made of white stuff around her neck.

"Excuse me," I asked them after we had exchanged pleasantries, "have you by any chance seen this woman?"

Taking the photo of my mother out from my wallet, I handed it to Mitzie, who was sitting to my left. She lowered a drink that smelled like ripe bananas and held the picture up to the light. "Hmm," she said, as if she were matching it to some file in her head, "are those fish?" She took out a pair of reading glasses to get a better look and wrinkled her small nose. "I don't think so . . . but wait . . ." She handed the picture to Carla, who had been telling me that she first joined the club after her husband died in a tragic accident involving—and here she had lowered her voice—what sounded like "a car wash." I was about to tell her about my father, when the stage was suddenly occupied by a woman more conservatively dressed than most of the other members in the audience around me. She wore a straight flowered skirt slit up the side and a ruffled crushed-silk red blouse, the top few buttons of which had been provocatively left undone. I assumed she was the president, or at least an officer of some high rank. Carla handed me back the picture of my mother. "I'll take a better look later when the lights go back on," she whispered, and squeezed my knee.

"Ladies," the woman on stage said in a smoker's contralto, "today I am sorry to say I have both good news and bad. The bad news is that the martial-arts presentation by the talented young men of the Sons of the Rising Sun Club has been canceled again. The good news is that at short notice I've been lucky enough to find the sort of high-class program that several of you have been requesting for a while now, namely a program with a serious educational component as well."

From the rear of the room I heard a groan, but I also noticed Carla tossing her red curls in satisfaction, and I wondered if the presence of the feather boa had caused me to underestimate her leanings of a more intellectual nature. She poked me playfully with a trident. "Oh, good," she whispered. "It's about time." There was a pause as the door behind me opened to admit a few latecomers. None of them looked a bit like my mother.

"And so today," our hostess went on, "we have the special pleasure of hearing from a speaker whom, if you have ever checked out a book at the main library where she works full time at the reference desk, you may already know. Yet even if you've met her in those mundane surroundings or heard her speak on other occasions as a spokesperson for that dynamic and spiritually oriented group the Fellowship of the Open Door, you still may be surprised by the topic she has chosen for us today. It is one that she says she has been quietly researching on her own for many years now: the very real possibility of sex after death."

The room erupted into confused applause and Doorperson Muriel appeared before me once again. She was still in her choir robe and matching turban. This time, I noticed, her arm was bandaged with a thick layer of gauze. Her left eye was mostly shut.

"Ladies of the Hot Club," she began, "I come to you today in the official uniform of the Fellowship of the Open Door, but this does not mean the ideas I am about to explore with you are those of the fellowship or its staff and management. No, today the opinions I am about to express are entirely my own."

The crowd stirred as Doorperson Muriel looked around. I wondered if she would recognize me. A few of the women squirmed in their seats, and I could feel the tension in the room increase. I noticed it rise inside me as well. For the first time, I began to speculate that there might be something about Doorperson Muriel's voice—some high-pitched vibration, undetectable by the human ear, like those that can set dogs howling—that had been responsible for awakening the violence that had followed her talk at the Rotary Lions. She began to hum beneath her breath while I considered this. Alternatively, it might also have been something about Doorperson Muriel herself—the angle of her body or the position of her elbows—that created in others a sixth sense in the same way we humans can unintentionally trigger the attack mechanisms of grizzly bears or great white sharks— maybe a particular order in the words of her sentences. I looked over at Mitzie. She seemed oblivious to any malign vibrations Doorperson Muriel might be emitting, and Carla appeared happy as well. Beneath the housecoat Carla was wearing a white slip, and she had on a pair of fluffy slippers, giving her feet an especially innocent quality. She caught my glance. She put a finger to her lips to indicate we would talk later.

Muriel continued, "I know you ladies have been criticized in the past, even by some of my fellow Doorpeople, for a certain narrowness in your interest regarding the spectrum on human activity—not that that's bad, by the way—but I'm here today to suggest that from what I've found, you may be surprisingly more correct than you can guess. I am here to tell you members of the Hot Club that an accumulating amount of evidence in my recent research is beginning to indicate that the grave, far from being the traditional place of quiet and passivity described by so much literature of the past, is nothing less than a hotbed of sexual activity—a real bonanza, in other words, for people like yourselves, who are shallow enough to be inclined in that direction."

Clearly, Muriel had gotten the ladies' attention. Mitzie moistened her lips with the tip of her tongue and winked at me.

Out of the corner of one eye I caught a flash of light. The door to the club had opened once again, briefly, admitting a newcomer, but I couldn't tell if the newcomer was my mother or not.

So I sat there and, as Doorperson Muriel's words blended into one another, found I was becoming more and more annoyed for no reason I could pinpoint. My throat felt dry,

After a small lifetime, I found myself blinking into the sudden dazzle of the street. I tried to catch a glimpse of whoever might have been fleeing, but in the process of my eyes adjusting from dark to all that light, I spotted no one. From inside the Hot Club came the now-familiar sounds of women shouting and the thumps of bodies hitting the floor.

Far in the distance I could hear the sound of an approaching police siren. From across the street a medium-sized brown dog watched me as if trying to guess whether I would leave the club or return. "He'll leave because he's not the kind to go back, even to help his new friends, Carla and Mitzie," I imagined the dog thinking, and the dog was right.

"Ouch," I said, because at that moment I was hit behind my ear by something either thrown or blown out of a passing black convertible; probably, I thought, someone in a hurry to arrive at a concert or a gallery opening. I picked it up. It was one of those deodorizers in the shape of a pine tree that people hang on their car mirror. This one was still in its plastic wrapper, and so was perfectly good. I stuck it in my shirt pocket. Maybe one day, I thought, if I ever got a car, I'd use it.

An hour later I was finally home and sitting in front of my window overlooking the Cuyahoga River. To help myself unwind from the day's excitement I resumed my work on a statue I had begun a week earlier, this one of Zeus's wife, Hera. It was strange to me, but with the whole world to choose from there was just something about those Greeks that called out for sculpting, and this time, to avoid the trouble I'd had with Athena, I'd started with the nares, taking care to make them as separate as I could. As I sculpted

I would look up every so often to watch the river flow by and to let its natural tranquillity flow into me, but the longer I worked, the more the statue of Hera began to resemble my mother, as if she had been lurking in the bag of EZ Sculpt all along, maybe even back in the days when it still rested on the shelf of Sunshine's husband's store, Jim's Art Supply, where all of her students automatically received a five-percent discount. A couple weeks into my lessons with Sunshine she had persuaded me to try EZ Sculpt. It was a lot more expensive than clay, but Sunshine said it was a far wiser choice for beginners. So I looked out the window at the river and then at the statue of what appeared to be my mother and then back out the window at the river, as if any minute a clue that solved everything would float by.

Be patient, I told myself, and I studied the sportsmen as they cast their shiny lures into the flowing, murky water, wound their lines back in, and then cast again, repeating this action ten, twenty, a hundred times without getting even a single strike. All at once I remembered the exact thing that seemed to be eluding me since I had arrived in Cleveland, the true message of Remindersville: every one of those lonely years growing up in St. Nils with Linda, each Christmas morning she would hand me a badly wrapped present battered by the mail and postmarked from this very city where I was now living.

"Here," Linda would say, "this is from your mother. Go ahead, let's see what she sent you this time; open it up." And then, when my child's hands finally managed to unstick the tape and untie the knots, I would find some fishing lure or other, a Daredevil painted red and white, a Jitterbug, a tape five

GUEST: (unintelligible) . . . the most amazing sense of lightness and joy, almost a frothy giddiness just to be there, not that I can say where *there* was, and to be speaking out loud and calling out like that, well not out loud, really, but communicating somehow, maybe through some sort of brain wave business, to others like me who were also inhabiting this space, if that's even what it was, because space and time at that point were pretty much completely mixed up, you know.

INTERVIEWER: And what about emotional depth? Was that sacrificed in the process you are describing, or was it somehow retained, Melanie?

GUEST: A good question, Warren, and fortunately the answer is both. Because, you see, the froth I'm describing is the result of the depth, like foam on the waves, so first you have the froth on top of the sea, but in order to have the froth you also have to have the sea as well, and the two of them combined are like some drink, let's say a good glass of beer with a really good head on it, though I know women aren't supposed to like beer, I actually do. Nor was I afraid in the least because that whole time I kept hearing some strange, built-in speakerphone device or headset that kept repeating in a deep voice, full of authority. It said, "You are not alone, Melanie. I will not abandon you. You and I are in this together because I have taken your mistakes from the past (and there were plenty of them, believe me) and have made them my mistakes, therefore it is impossible for me to mock you or to judge you, no matter how stupid your conclusions have been, Melanie, because, you see, I myself have arrived at the same stupid conclusions at the same time as you, if you follow me. And not only that, as for future errors, you are also covered because I will be there as well to witness the dumb things you are about to do at any minute." So, hearing that, it was hard to feel too bad, or much of anything in general.

INTERVIEWER: That's remarkable. So you're telling me that you didn't feel alone out there, wherever *there* was?

GUEST: Exactly, Warren. Far from it. I don't know how to say it. I don't know how to talk about this feeling of being cared for. It happened about three years ago at a party at someone's house. I walked into a glass sliding door that I hadn't realized was closed because, you know, I'd had a little too much to drink, and suddenly there I was, lying on the floor right next to a heaping bowl of dry cat food, confused, and maybe nearly unconscious—at any rate things were fading in and out—while all around me the party was still going on, completely unabated, and that's when I heard the voice that said I wasn't alone.

INTERVIEWER: So there you were.

GUEST: There I was, yes, and amazingly, right after that a pleasant gentleman who was a complete stranger to me at that time walked up and dragged me to a couch. Then he said, "Just stay here until you feel better, my dear." Afterward, he drove me home to his place.

INTERVIEWER: And after that, Melanie?

GUEST: After that things pretty much went back to normal.

10

woke from a dream in which I was a trout darting out from beneath my sunken log only to bite down on a clever imitation of a minnow and be pulled in toward a rowboat with a bucket full of concrete for an anchor and a number on its side. I woke in a cold sweat, made myself a cup of coffee, ate a couple of those jelly donuts—cold—and went back to work on Hera's forehead.

It was true: Hera was looking more like my mother every minute, but, artistically speaking, I couldn't decide whether this was a good or bad thing. On the one hand, it might mean that I was destined to be forever second-rate, a derivative artist at best and not a real creator, but on the other, didn't all those classic sculptors work from models? I needed to remember to ask Sunshine. Besides, if I was channeling the image of my mother through my imagination, couldn't that mean that the source of my inspiration was deep and to be reckoned with? Or was I only using my mother's graven image for a surrogate successful conclusion to my quest? Was a statue even close to the real thing? Would I ever find my mother here in Cleveland? Did I have any aptitude as a sculptor? Sunshine claimed I did, but was her nearly constant praise only a ploy to keep me signing up for new lessons? Should I start a serious exercise program? (I'd been putting on quite a few pounds since I'd discovered those donuts.) Also, several of my fellow students had told me that the prices at Jim's Art Supply, even with the discount, were nearly double that of some of the chain stores. Was Jim taking advantage of his connection with Sunshine to make an obscene profit from the students who trusted her, not only on EZ Sculpt but on other materials as well? Did Sunshine know this was going on? I could see that the world of art, so placid on its surface, was filled with many a troubling current and treacherous eddy. So these and other such thoughts whirled through my mind until they were suddenly halted midcerebellum by a knock on the door. I opened it, and there stood Uleene.

"Where have you been? I've been trying to get in touch with you," I said.

"Ted, honey," she said, "let me in. There's something important I have to tell you."

My heart jumped. "Is it about my mom?"

"Not exactly." Uleene looked around like one of those characters in a movie who's afraid that someone is listening to them from behind every door, even though at that moment they are up on a screen being overheard and seen by hundreds of strangers. "Sarge has disappeared."

"Sarge . . ." I said, and it took me a heartbeat to remember who Sarge was. "Sarge as in Sarge's Bait? Sarge of Aurora Pond? That Sarge? What happened?"

Uleene put a finger to her lips as a signal for me to be quiet for a moment. She glanced down the stairs behind her to check if she had been followed, but the stairway was empty. She walked to the front window, looked up and down the street, and, finding nothing suspicious, returned to me. "It was in the newspaper this morning," she said. "Two nights ago, by all accounts, Sarge was working late, hosing out the bottoms of his boats and getting his Styrofoam cups of worms ready for the next day. He'd had a few beers, but no more than usual. Then the next morning, when the first fishermen arrived, they pounded on the door of the bait shack thinking he was sleeping one off as sometimes happened, but no one answered. Finally, one of the fishermen chanced to turn around to look at the pond to see if the fish were biting, and what did he see? He saw one of Sarge's boats, old Number Eight, just floating out there, and not even over any good fishing spot but drifting all over the place. Its oars were dead in the water, and its anchor was completely missing."

"You seem unusually upset," I said. "Why?"

"I *am* upset," she answered, "and you can't possibly understand. Remember, I told you I had issues with most men"—had she? I couldn't remember—"but you should also know that Sarge was both the reason for several of those issues and an exception to the general rule. You see, while for most people Sarge is only a bad-smelling, gruff-talking, foul-breathing, hard-drinking, overweight, opinionated, narrow-minded, intolerant, ex-military man with a bad case of the shakes, the fact is that Sarge and I have a history. He wasn't always the way you saw him the other day. You should have met him not all that long ago, when he was forceful and dynamic and full of love for nature and nature's ways."

"How did you know that I went out to the pond and saw Sarge the other day?" I asked.

"Sometimes," she said, "we talk."

"Talk! Why talk?"

"Yes, talk. You see, Theodore, not that long ago I was fresh out of the state pen and things were pretty shaky for me. I knew I wanted to help people who were in trouble—that was why we'd started Satan's Samaritans—I just wasn't sure how to do it. So one day I was out on the road by myself with El Diablo, blowing the carbon out of its pistons, when my eye caught a sign on a telephone pole I was passing. It read *Lost Kittie*.

"Well, naturally, I slowed El Diablo and wheeled it back to the sign, where I dismounted and retrieved a pencil and a brown stenographer's notebook from one of my saddlebags. It was upsetting that they had spelled *kitty* with an *ie* and had not given her a name, but I copied the number anyway. As I did I was surprised to hear a small meowing coming from a tall clump of grass about six feet away from the pole. Could it be the very kitten in question? At first I dismissed the possibility as too much of a coincidence, but when I thought about it, I realized that, obviously, the family would have put up their misspelled notices in areas where they expected the kitten to be found, and not in places where there was absolutely no chance for success. I walked to the clump of grass, and sure enough, there was a small black kitten huddled in a pocket of stalks.

"So I picked up the kitten, a pathetic-looking thing, put it in my saddlebag, and sped back to my apartment, where I planned to call its owners and tell them I had found their missing pet. Horribly, however, when I opened my saddle-bag I found the kitten lying there, unmoving. It had probably been just barely alive when I found it, and the ride back to my apartment must have pushed it over the edge. I felt terrible, but what was done was done. So with a heart full of sadness I called the number on the notice and left a message telling them that their pet had expired in my saddlebag and I was really sorry. But when they returned my call, instead of a reward, or even thanks, I was amazed to hear that not only were they blaming me but they also claimed that I had murdered their kitten deliberately. They said they had my name, which I had foolishly left on my message, and told me that they planned to prosecute me under the full extent of the law unless I paid them this huge sum of money."

Uleene went back to the window and checked outside to see if there was anyone suspicious standing outside the building.

"Of course, this sort of misadventure happens to people every day, and there's usually no harm done, but, remember, I was fresh out of prison and still on probation. I was not in the best position to defend myself. So in order to make myself feel better, I decided to spend a day out on the calm waters of Aurora Pond. I took a fishing pole and jumped on El Diablo and eventually made my way into the shack to buy some bait. Sarge was there, and it was a quiet morning so we began to talk, then one thing led to another. I told him about the problems I was having with the vengeful cat-owning family, and he just looked me straight in the eye. 'You give me their number,' he said, and grabbed the phone.

"Within minutes, through a combination of masterful cross-examination and actual physical threats, he got the family to admit that the kitten that had died was a different animal entirely than their pet, which the family had found cowering under their front porch a couple days previous to my call. I'd never met a man more masterful, and even though I had heard he was married, she had left him—for good, he said—so I guess we had what you'd call a fling. In the end, though, he told me he had other fish to fry."

She paused, "And now, along with your mother, Sarge is missing."

I looked around my apartment. About fifty yards past my front window the river flowed on its way to one of the smaller of the Great Lakes. Behind me, the sun above the top of the metal-fabricating plant down the street was just peeking through my kitchen window. On my kitchen counter the toaster still innocently gleamed next to a patch of crumbs like a chrome elephant amid a tribe of pygmies. My half-opened bathroom door revealed a roll of scented toilet paper waiting patiently to be pulled from inside its recessed holder in the tiled wall and put to use. My slippered feet were planted on the mostly blue rag rug that had come with the place. In several of the corners of the room I noticed dust balls. A cobweb was hanging off the light. In other words, I hadn't been there that long, and the place already needed a cleaning.

"Where have you been?" I asked her again. "I called several times lately but you never answered your phone."

"Ted, honey, I can't talk about that right now. Suffice it to say that I have a life of my own; there are others out there besides you who also need my help, although I am willing to concede few if any are as messed up as you."

It was strange. Nothing had really changed since the time I'd gotten up to answer the door and opened it to find Uleene standing there, and yet everything had changed. It appeared that Sarge, whom I had scarcely known, but who had perhaps carried the key to the mystery of my mother, was gone, and the ripples of his disappearance had been carried straight to me across the trembling surface of the metaphorical pond of Uleene, who was now vulnerable in a way that I had never seen her.

"Would you like a cup of coffee?" I asked. "You look as if you could use some steadying yourself."

"Sorry, yes," she said, and followed me to the kitchen, where I made a cup of instant coffee. Uleene sat at the table and rubbed her forehead with the palm of her hand until a red spot appeared.

"Cream and sugar?"

"Both," she answered.

"Uleene," I said, "you can let it all out."

She took a sip and began to speak in a rambling pastiche

that combined bits of her personal history; references to various feminist tracts; her past; her own deadbeat father, whom Sarge apparently had replaced in her mind for a time; highlights from several situation comedies that had recently aired on television; a short, but what seemed mostly a well-reasoned critique of the criminal justice system; a few tips on how to survive in a women's prison, should I ever find myself in one; certain points of interest that she believed I might have missed since I'd arrived in Cleveland; descriptions of numerous drug trips, both pleasant and bad, she had taken as a youth; her opinions on the merits of competing brands of motorcycles; humorous stories involving various members of the Cleveland police department; and several phrases she claimed were well-known aphorisms, none of which I had ever heard—all of these punctuated with various items of celebrity gossip she'd gleaned from supermarket tabloids over the past several months.

At last her monologue trailed off into silence, and I realized that she had completely left out the circumstances of how she came to be in prison in the first place. I would have enjoyed hearing her story in a completely nonjudgmental way if she wished to share it, but I knew that if Uleene wanted to talk about it, she would—I wasn't about to bring it up—I understood that much about women. I stared at her. She seemed to have yet one more thing to say, something she was reluctant to tell me.

"What's the deal?" I said. "Spit it out."

There was a long pause during which Uleene put her finger on the tabletop and traced several mysterious patterns. "The deal is that when they went to look for Sarge and didn't find him, instead they found a tackle box with your mother's name, Helen, written on top in Magic Marker."

It was my turn to pause. "Mom's tackle box? How did they know it was my mother's and that it didn't belong to one of Sarge's former one-night stands (no offense, Uleene) who just happened to share my mother's name?"

"Easy. It had her old fishing license inside. Plus a picture of you, Ted, as a preteen that she had pasted to the inner lid. You were kind of cute back then, by the way, and quite a bit thinner."

"I don't get it," I said. "What was her connection to Sarge? Did the fact that she had my picture pasted to the lid of her tackle box mean that she *had* cared about me? Had Linda been sending her pictures of me without my knowledge the whole time I was growing up? Why did my mother leave St. Nils in such a hurry? Does anyone else know that it's my picture? Where is my mother now? Where did those postcards come from? And finally, is my mother—as impossible as it sounds—still alive?"

Uleene was silent for a long while and sipped her coffee. "I don't exactly know the answers to most of your questions," she finally answered, "but let me fill you in on what I do know: From the account in the *Plain Dealer* of the whole Sarge-missing-person-business, after your mom returned to Cleveland several months ago one of the first things she did was to join the Fish Wives, a short-lived club that fell apart over the question of chumming. There's no telling, really, exactly how long her tackle box had been there. Nor do I know if Sarge was just keeping it for her, or if he had taken it as a souvenir in the way that certain creepy guys keep a souvenir from every girl they've ever made love to. Sarge wasn't actually creepy, but he did have a reputation, I'll admit that."

Mom and Sarge together. I pictured the man I had watched as he dozed in his lawn chair, and then I pictured my mother.

"What do you mean, 'chumming'?" I asked.

"I mean whether or not it's ethical to attract fish by throwing things like bread crumbs and ground pork, even sacks of dried blood, into the water, so that after the fish have dropped their guard to stuff themselves with free eats, they can easily be hooked on a worm or a lure."

"Is there anything I can do to help the police find my mother, being as I'm already on the case, so to speak?"

"I don't see how," she said. "When it comes to it, what do you have? Only two postcards somebody sent you, and you can't really even prove they were from Helen. It could even be that somebody else's mother with the same name addressed them to you by mistake, though I have to admit that doesn't sound likely. Too bad that Sarge couldn't stay around to talk to you before he disappeared."

I began to ask her again what she and Sarge had been talking about during their last talk, but Uleene put up her hand. "Listen, Theodore, I told you I'm upset, and I am, but that's as far as I'm willing to go. I guess all you can really do is to just keep hoping that you'll find a clue somewhere, and really soon, one that actually turns out to be important."

I thought about it. Did I have any clues? I shook my head no, but I looked around anyway. Lying next to the shelf where I kept my sculpting tools, I saw the pine-scented car deodorizer I'd been struck by on the way back from the Hot Club. It was still in its clear cellophane wrapper. I held it out to Uleene.

"The only thing I have that could remotely be a clue is this." I shrugged. "It flew out of some speeding vehicle, a convertible, and probably the owner is still looking for it under his seats or floor mats. Either that or he threw it at me."

"My God," Uleene said. "Do you know what you are holding in your hand at this very moment?"

"A car deodorizer?"

"Yes," she replied, "but that so-called deodorizer happens also to be the emblem for the Christmas Tree Club. This could be exactly the break you need."

"The Christmas Tree Club," I said wonderingly. "I've never heard of it. What on earth is the Christmas Tree Club?"

"The Christmas Tree Club is only the most notorious women's club in Cleveland, Ted," Uleene said. "There's a lot that people say about it, some of it good, and plenty not so good. I'd rather let you decide for yourself, especially if it turns out that your mom is still alive and involved with that bunch. You'll have to find out when their next meeting is and then see if you can find a way to attend. It's supposed to be nearly impossible for strangers to get in, and I'm afraid I won't be able to come with you. I don't even know where they're hanging out these days. I seem to remember them being kicked out of the last few places where they've held their meetings."

"Well, OK," I said, "but if it's so bad and everything, how do you know so much about it?"

Uleene gave me a funny look. "Back when I was in prison," she answered, "one of the matrons who had a crush on me was a member."

11

CLEARLY ULEENE KNEW

more than she was telling me, but what? Had the disappearance of Sarge driven her into some private place, or was she protecting me in some way? I couldn't tell. Whichever it was, it seemed important. I looked in the phone book but there was no listing for the Christmas Tree Club. I picked up the *Plain Dealer* and found the article Uleene had mentioned on page seventeen. What she said was true; there it was in black and white.

And there I was, sipping my coffee, dipping my stale donuts into it to soften them, trying to sort all this new information into digestible piles, when the phone rang. It was Marty back in St. Nils. He said another murder had taken place, this time using one of our basswood-handled trowels, and the result was that our customers seemed to have passed the thrill-of-purchasing-a–potential-murder-weapon state and were starting to become frightened. Marty told me that sales were down, way down, so much so that he wouldn't be sending me a check that month, and I didn't know whether to believe him or if there was something else I needed to look into. He sounded nervous. He wanted to know if I would be coming back any time soon. I knew I probably should go back immediately, but the precise moment that I actually had begun to find out some information about my mother seemed to be exactly the wrong time to leave. There was something about the simple shape of that hurled air freshener, or maybe something about the words *Christmas Tree Club* that sent shivers down my back, as if the two together added up to something more—to my mother.

"Let me think about it," I told Marty. "Hold down the fort. Keep me posted. Hang in there."

I thought I could hear a sigh of relief on the other end of the phone. "Sure," Marty said. "No problem. I just didn't want you to worry that I was taking funds from your account or anything like that. Ha, ha. Just joking."

I walked downstairs and asked Raul if he'd ever heard of the Christmas Tree Club. "Oh that," he said. "Sure, but I had always assumed it was just the sort of ugly rumor that surfaces from time to time, then disappears." I went back upstairs to my apartment and, over another cup of coffee, read the rest of the *Plain Dealer*. "Rats Back!" the headline shouted. The article that followed went on to explain that because of the disappointing results of the last campaign, of which the total kill had been a mere twenty-seven ("the indifference of a happy citizenry?"), and the simple fact that those rats who survived (most of them, obviously) had slightly less competition for food, therefore a few more minutes each day to copulate, their numbers were larger than ever.

The previous day, according to the article, a pack of adolescent Norwegian browns had attacked a cellist on his way home from an orchestra rehearsal. The cellist had escaped unhurt, but the cello, a Strad, had been badly savaged by the rats' strong young teeth.

As a result, the mayor had called for one more effort by the citizens of Cleveland, in his words, "to eradicate the terror of rats from our city once and for all." "The War Against Rat Terror," as he dubbed it, would take place exactly one week from that morning. I thought about my responsibility in the matter. This city had been good to me, and even if I was soon to return to St. Nils, it seemed ungracious to abandon it just because the first skirmish in the war had been a dud. I was not a quitter. I had not given up searching for my mother, and I would give rat hunting another try as well.

The phone rang again. It was Sunshine, who also had read the article. "This is the real thing, Theodore, I can feel it in my bones," she said. "Be there."

I searched for an address for the Christmas Tree Club at the library, the city hall, and at the Department of Social Services, all without results, though one person in social services gave me a funny look when I asked her.

On the morning of the commencement of the "war," I answered the knock on my door to see Sunshine standing there once again, wearing a new pair of high-topped boots but, somewhat to my surprise, without her polo mallet.

"Together again," she said, and thrust out to me a gleaming, official Little League bat crafted from red anodized aluminum. "I hope you don't mind, Ted, but I was getting one for myself, and I thought why not bring you a present." She showed me her own full-sized wooden Louisville Slugger. "This is mine," she said. "After that unsatisfactory last rat hunt, I was hanging around talking with some aficionados down at the Diamond Bar and Grill, and they convinced me that a polo mallet, while pretty sporting, really isn't the best thing. They said I might miss the blood, but a genuine Slugger like this one makes a much more satisfying sound—and they're right." She thumped it against the side of her boot to demonstrate. Then she walked over to where the as-yet unfinished sculpture of Hera was resting on its pedestal by the window. "Nice nostrils," she said. "Are you ready to go?"

"As ready as ever," I told her. "By the way, have you ever heard of the Christmas Tree Club?"

"Hmm," Sunshine said. "I might have, but I'm afraid I'm drawing a blank at the moment."

We walked onto the street, past the line of customers waiting for Love Hurts to open its doors. Sunshine looked at them with disapproval. "I guess some people can't be bothered with such minor things as public health and the destruction of priceless instruments of classical music," she said. The day was clear, and the wind was blowing toward us from the north, off the lake.

"Rat weather," Sunshine remarked.

So we strolled in the crisp morning breeze, hefting our bats, Sunshine and I, but we saw no rodents of any sort.

Then we joined a group of other hunters, a couple of whom I recognized from the various classes I had taken before I'd discovered Sunshine's sculpture class. Our group wielded our clubs, shouted, joined another group of rat hunters, and then another group, all without seeing even a single rat. It was heartening to see Cleveland's inhabitants respond in such numbers this time around, but I was starting to feel discouraged once again.

"I thought today was supposed to be different. Do you think it's the size of our group, which I estimate to be about three hundred, that has frightened them away?" I asked Sunshine.

"Naw," she said. "I've heard stories of rats approaching even larger groups and never batting an eye." But she seemed less sure of herself in this regard, and maybe even anxious.

And so, like an immense, deadly-to-rats snowball, we rolled forward, gathering up more and more people, some with city-issued clubs, others with baseball bats, others with hockey sticks, croquet mallets, tennis rackets, golf clubs, and even ping-pong paddles—banging on trash can lids and shouting—all without seeing even a single rodent. It was surprising, I thought—when I looked around at all the equipment people had brought with them—how many sports seemed to have been conceived with their primary purpose to practice killing small animals.

We passed a monument to fallen soldiers, one to drowned sailors, one to downed airmen, and even one for a group of conscientious objectors whose hospital laundry room had blown up due to a faulty thermostat. We passed statues of former mayors, former councilmen, former teachers-of-the-year, students-of-the-month, newspaper boys who had been lost in the snowdrifts of winter and not found until the following spring, the funniest dog and the most intelligent swine, and the fastest horse and most-milk-producing cow, but we saw no rats at all.

Then, rounding a corner, I began to feel the prickly sensation that I've heard people describe as a precursor to the presence of the supernatural. I looked up from the gutters and trash heaps where I'd been searching out vermin without success, and that's when I saw them, silhouetted on the horizon just as those Indians, war-painted and wearing headdresses and silent on their ponies, used to pause in Western movies atop some bluff beneath which the wagon train was due to travel, awaiting a sign from their chief to swoop down on the hapless pioneers, who, ignorant of Native American habits and customs, more than likely had been churning through miles of sacred burial grounds, the wheels of their wagons unearthing whole villages of corpses as well as turning up sacks of really valuable artifacts along the way, had they only known. Except, of course, we were no band of pioneers, and they, being only rats, were not on ponies.

Still, the rats held their own ground, silent, many on their hind legs, waving their small paws and curling back their lips as if, in their limited rat minds, they actually believed that the sight of so many incisors bared all at once might somehow strike a chord of terror in us humans and make us rethink our mission. *Oh foolish rats*, I thought, *when have humans ever rethought anything?* But then I wondered how long they had stood gathered there like that. Had they somehow gotten word of Rat Day Two ahead of time (the news wasn't exactly a secret, but how would *they* have known?), or was it just that, seeing the threatening hordes of humans armed with lethal sports equipment, through some miracle of instinctive organizational skill, the canny rodents had sent out word via whatever communication channels were available to those without technology and had joined together to counterattack.

All at once, as if at an invisible signal, they began a high-pitched, almost musical squeal that I took as either a battle cry or a cry for mercy. All of the rats—the old, the adolescents, even some with young children, making this as-musical-as-it-may-have-been-to-them, earsplitting-to-me sound, as if to say: "What now? What are you accusing us of that you would yourselves not have done? Is it so very wrong that we find food for ourselves and for our families? Is it so wrong that we love and, as a consequence along with the Universal Law of Life, reproduce? Is it our collective fault that we scurry out of the way to seek shelter when attacked by a far-larger foe? Yes, we know our tails are hairless as opposed to those of squirrels, which for some reason you humans seem to find attractive, even going so far as to bring bags of nuts to them in parks and cemeteries while all we rats do is mostly give you the creeps, but have you ever once thought that this may only be because you yourselves are mostly hairless and don't wish to be reminded of that fact? And surely," the rats seemed to be keening from on high, "though at this moment you humans as a species find yourselves at what you, in your limited wisdom, believe is the top of the evolutionary ladder, really, how long can that last? Why not show a little mercy, you So-called Intelligent Ones, because you will not always be where you are now, on top of the food chain, and when that time comes, you'll need a little mercy shown yourselves?"

I attempted to put my fingers in my ears, but to do that and keep hold of my bat was too difficult.

"And by the way," the rats continued, "naturally we're as devastated as you are over the destruction of the Stradivarius, but how much great stuff have *you*, both as a race and as individuals, tossed out in the trash only to see it turning up later on one of those Antique Road Show programs? It's the nature of time to destroy things, remember. Oh, and speaking of destruction, we don't suppose you'll be wanting to give advice on how to raise adolescents, now, will you, you who have been so successful with your own?

"Also along those lines (and forgive us, people, if our address to you seems to be jumping around a bit, but we're under a lot of stress at this moment): Regarding the damaged cello, please remember that the man will play again. On the other hand, in our case, *you* seem bent on our total extermination, without even taking a second to contemplate all the nasty memories this ought to be activating in you concerning your own murderous history. Which isn't to say we don't have our own fighting skills, mind you, so even if we lose, there are bound to be human casualties.

"People"—the rats seemed to be saying—"for the last time, listen to reason. Even now it's not too late. We can work things out. How many chromosomes is it that separate us? Four? Eight? We can't be certain because we're only rats, but we're positive it's not that many. And for that matter what's so bad about rats getting in the garbage every once in a while? Eliminate us, and you'll still have the garbage, along with flies, and probably even more flies than ever in that case because without us there will just be more garbage for the flies to eat. Also, concerning that old wives' tale about us spreading disease, as you well know, the chief vectors for human disease are humans, and even with the black plague, an admittedly unfortunate time, it wasn't us alone. It was fleas that infested humans as well as rats, remember?"

During this squealed monologue I noticed the rats were steadily creeping closer until, by the time they had finished, they were no longer just a thin, gray line on the horizon, but were practically at our feet, an endless carpet of small yellow incisors and scratchy brown claws.

Suddenly, from somewhere to my left I heard a sickening thwack, and without even thinking I lifted up my own bat, gleaming in the midday sun.

And held it suspended there.

What would my mother say, I thought, *if she were somehow here watching me now?*—and indeed she might have been; it was a big crowd. She had been a sportswoman, and while it was true her prey had been limited to the finny variety, nonetheless I wondered if her own experience of death (if she *was* dead) had contributed to any change in her perspective. Because what exact difference would the death of one, or two, or twenty rats possibly make to me, who, as all men, must find my own death in time? And even if it *did* make a difference, how could I possibly articulate what that difference would be? There was life and there was death. There was my former existence as the owner of a small business and my current one as a novice sculptor in Cleveland. Once I had a mother; now I could not seem to find her. Once I had a small but pleasant house in St. Nils; now I lived above a sex shop across from a brown river. Yesterday there was no sea of rats spread before me; now there was an endless ocean of the vermin. Yes, true enough, all right—but other than that, had anything really changed? The bottom line was that I was still living alone and still, somewhere on the other end of the continent, my gardening implement business was either going bankrupt or not. Also, I had yet to discover the whereabouts of my own mother, and now, on top of everything else, Sarge had gone missing.

Suddenly I was sickened by the futility of the whole endless process of human endeavor. Living or dead, the difference between life and death seemed only the difference between standing on one's right foot or one's left. At that moment, however, I was standing on *both*, in a new city, and being asked, albeit ever so nicely, by its leaders to send some rats to "the other side," where quite possibly Sarge himself, and my mother, too, might already be lurking. Baseball bat upraised, I stared into the panicked, beady eyes of a small brownish-gray animal at my feet. It was a heavily pregnant mother.

"Ted Bellefontaine," she seemed to be saying, "it's your call, brother."

I tapped Sunshine lightly on the shoulder to get her attention.

"Sunshine," I said. "Take back the bat. I can't do it."

Sunshine appeared not to understand, but took the Little League implement from me, swinging it a few times in a quizzical fashion, as if there were something wrong with it and perhaps it needed fixing.

"No, Sunshine," I told her. "The bat is just fine. It's perfect, Sunshine. It's a real beauty, and I thank you for bringing it for me today. It's just that I can't go through with this cruel charade for a minute longer."

Sunshine looked from me, to the rats, and then to the bat. Slowly, I saw a light flicker on in her exceptionally large head, as if before her very eyes a new possibility for human behavior had just been invented, one that might, if she could but follow it, free her from the endless chain of cause and effect, of action and reaction, followed by yet more action, the same chain that had imprisoned her and the rest of humankind as well for all our days on earth.

Flickered, and then went out.

"Whatever," she said. "What's wrong with you anyway, Ted? Are you some kind of a momma's boy?" Then Sunshine raised her Slugger high and got down to the bloody business at her feet.

I walked away, doubting everything I had ever heard about the so-called gentling effect of art. Or, if such a thing *did* exist, what must Clevelanders have been like before its infusion? Down one mean street and up another I strode, trying to decide if it were possible to separate the behavior of the artist from the works of exquisite beauty he or she might create. Certainly the history of art was littered with murderers, thugs, wastrels, liars, gluttons, and probably ratbashers, but nonetheless . . .

And then, I was lost. I turned here and there, and none of it seemed to make sense until, without knowing quite how, I found myself in a part of the city unknown to me, one that looked as if it were in the middle of some sort of renewal project. A wrecking ball hung pensively from a crane, its operator having taken the day off, I supposed, to hunt rats. Several buildings around the crane had been reduced to mounds of bricks and conduit and plasterboard, while others waited with exposed beams and missing roofs. The only place for blocks that was left intact was a sort of bunker-looking building dug into the earth. It had a reinforced roof, coils of barbed wire, and sandbags pushed against its walls.

It was just possible, I thought, that someone was still living there, and if so they might give me directions on how to return to Love Hurts as quickly as possible. I raised the heavy old-fashioned knocker and let it fall with a thud.

No one answered.

Fall, thud, nothing.

Fall, thud, nothing.

I turned to leave, but then, as I did, I chanced to see stuck into a small brass frame to the left of the door a piece of paper the size of a business card:

THE CHRISTMAS TREE CLUB
MEETS ON THE FIRST FRIDAY OF THE MONTH
4 PM SHARP

As luck (and it was about time) would have it, the first Friday of the month was only a week away. All I needed to do was remember where this place was, go home, and return the next Friday. Far, very far away in the distance, I could hear the faint screams of rats grow even fainter. Should I make my way back to them, or attempt to find my apartment on my own? I took my bearings so as to be sure I could return to where I was, and then, for the second time, luck struck. Just as I was making up my mind in which direction to point myself, I was approached by an elderly gentleman wearing a trench coat.

"Excuse me," I said, "you wouldn't happen to know the way to Love Hurts, would you?"

It turned out he knew the way very well indeed.

tape six

INTERVIEWER: But this whole sign thing I still find really confusing. It seems so strange. You are telling me, Franklin, that there are certain signs?

GUEST: Of course there are, Suzanne. Otherwise there's no way I could have gotten as far as I did. This wasn't an easy or a simple journey, this trip, and I only hope that the people who buy my book will be able to make use of it for themselves so as not to get completely lost the way I did for a while myself. Such an experiment as mine is not something to be taken without serious preparation by any traveler. That's why I say the first step is to learn to recognize the signs that you will see along the way, which are laid out in greater detail, of course, in my book.

INTERVIEWER: And the nature of the signs—if you could explain that a bit more to us, please.

GUEST: Oh, they're ordinary enough all right—like "This Way," and "Rest Here," and "Right Turn," but what is different about each one is the lettering and the coloring.

INTERVIEWER: That's so very interesting. If the words are in green, for example, what would that mean?

GUEST: It would mean several things, actually, depending on the typeface as well. As I said, Suzanne, people have to buy my book for a full understanding, but just to give you an example, though it's oversimplified, of course, if the sign were in green, say an ordinary Times Roman, so as not to complicate things, in the first place that would indicate there were no other colors present: there would be no red, for example.

INTERVIEWER: And what would that mean?

GUEST: Several things, as I said, but physiologically, for example, and specifically concerning the cells of the optic nerve, it would mean that in your average death situation some of the cells that recognize color might well expire before others, so depending on the color—I didn't know this at the time, naturally—by the use of color a person can mark exactly where he or she is in the process. I mean, of course, the dying one.

INTERVIEWER: In which case the end is signaled by . . .?

GUEST: Black and white, I suppose, though, as I said, I didn't get along that far myself. The farthest I got was a sort of periwinkle blue in Perpetua Italic.

INTERVIEWER: And then?

GUEST: And then it started to fade. I don't know if you've ever seen a printer's blue line when it's exposed to the sun, but it was like that, so for a minute I wasn't worried about being dead at all, only that I was going blind. And that was when I started to run, to get somewhere before I lost my sight completely, and kept on running. The very last thing I remember was a smallish yellow sign, not much bigger than an index card, with yellow letters in Optima Bold, that said, "Bridge this Way," with an arrow, and honestly, even though I had no idea what that bridge was or where it was going to, I headed toward it as fast as I could.

INTERVIEWER: I can't say as I blame you. And it took you where?

GUEST: Why, Suzanne, it took me to your radio studio, with my book, naturally.

12

ALL IN ALL, I HAD TO
say the bust of Hera turned out pretty well.

After the sculpture spent a while being my mother, and then a short time as Marie Curie, and right after that dived into Uleene, at the very last moment it returned to the classic mode and looked like no one in particular, unless it was a combination of all three. It had taken most of the week between the War Against Rat Terror and the day before the meeting of the Christmas Tree Club to get it that way, but when I finally carried it through the doorway of the store Sunshine rented for her studio and removed the red and white checked tablecloth I'd wrapped around it, Sunshine said, "My Goodness. Maybe it's time you started thinking about having a major show of your work. Not that I expect you'll sell anything at first, mind you. That's seldom the case for beginning artists, but it might be interesting for you to see how your work stacks up against the work of seasoned professionals in the field. Whoever this is, she looks both helpful and full of vengeance, but with a touch of the scientific spirit of inquiry as well. When it comes to finding a gallery, you'll be glad to know that Jim has an extra room behind his art supply store that I'm sure he will let you rent at a reasonable rate."

Sunshine moved Hera off to a storage area ("the place of honor," she said) to keep it safe. "Theodore," she said, "I know that you missed the end of the rat hunt, which turned into a real mission accomplished, but don't feel bad. I expect these rat hunts are an acquired taste, and some people, like Jim, never seem to get it. But I hope that if you stay in Cleveland, you'll change your mind. Don't worry, you'll have other chances; this is Cleveland, after all."

The following afternoon I found my way back to the neighborhood of the Christmas Tree Club and was happy to see the trench-coated old gentleman was still there, still active. He must have lived in the area, though I couldn't imagine where, amid all that rubble.

It was shortly after four when, breathless and embarrassed by my tardiness, I reached the door of the Christmas Tree Club's bunker. A stocky woman in a green blouse and skirt stood outside. In her right eyebrow was a small, silver ring. She shifted from side to side, as if preparing to find a spot to wrestle me to the ground. "I'm sorry I'm late," I told her, "even if it's only by a couple of minutes, and I want you to know I mean no disrespect."

"Don't you know this club is for women, sonny?" she asked me.

"Yes," I said, "and that's exactly why I'm here. I have it on good authority that my mother is a member of this club, and she asked me to be here today, for this very meeting."

At the word *authority* the doorperson came a bit more to life. "And what is your mother's name, please?"

"Helen Bellefontaine. Has she already arrived?"

"I don't know. That name sounds slightly familiar, but I cannot place her face. I'm sorry, but you will have to go away unless you can bring the proper documents," she said. "These include, but are not limited to, a letter written on Christmas Tree Club stationery signed by a member of the club, in this case, your mother, if she is, as you say, such."

I was desperate. "Well then," I stabbed, "maybe you know another friend of mine, Uleene Trail. She also told me I absolutely had to be here today."

At Uleene's name the woman straightened up. I don't know what she knew about Uleene, but the name carried more weight than I'd expected. The heavy woman disappeared inside, and then returned after several minutes. "Here," she said, and handed me a heavy paper brochure. "I told you this club is not in general open to men, and that you also need a letter, signed, as I have instructed, but an exception to the rule I will make this once. I don't suppose a single time can do any harm. Tell Uleene that Gretel says hello." She opened the door and I entered.

The formidable bunker in which the Christmas Tree Club met was painted red and green. It smelled strongly of pine, probably not from any of the actual trees present (there were five scrubby ones in plastic pots) but thanks to about five hundred air fresheners similar to the one that had caught me in that tender spot just behind my ear, following the Hot Club debacle. These, however, hung from the rafters. There were no windows.

The podium, situated off to one side on the far end of the bunker, continued the color scheme with a wrapping of red and green crepe paper and sported what I took to be the club's other symbol, a sort of a plus sign, the ends of which were all bent counterclockwise at a ninety-degree angle and which the brochure described as "a druidic symbol of forest life." Running down the bent-up cross was a lightning bolt, the symbol, the brochure also explained, for "change and inspiration." I took a seat near the back and to one side. As I waited, I glanced through the rest of the surprisingly lengthy brochure.

Begun in Germany following the dark days of the Second World War by a former secretary to a high-ranking National Socialist Party official, its founder, Frau Greta Schmidt, had, not without bitterness, put aside the failed ideology of fascism to return to her roots as a druid. In the words of the brochure: "Out of all trees, it is the Christmas one that, through its fresh scent, broad base, and prickly boughs narrowing as they reach toward heaven, symbolizes the spiritual regeneration needed, not just by former Nazis, but by all mankind." At the same time, the text went on to explain, the tree's increasingly pointed and eventually finite top was also an excellent reminder that not everyone who strived would achieve her or his goal. While many might try, these penultimate branches had only a limited amount of space for ornaments, no matter how bright. Consequently, there would only be a chosen few seekers of a superior sort who would be admitted to this highest level, and these seekers would consist entirely of women. "The men had their chance earlier to kick the ball through the net of history," the brochure read, "and they missed their free shot at the penalty kick when they decided to invade the Soviet Union."

I looked around the bunker. It was lit by torches sticking out from the walls. In the dodgy light I couldn't see my mother anywhere, so I turned back to the brochure, which, following a montage of photos from the invasion of Poland ("The Good War"), asked rhetorically, "And to express this important message did our Creator choose the redwood, with its top so far away it can't even be reached, let alone brought into a house and set in front of the fireplace to be hung with decorations made by children in countless elementary school art classes all over the land?"

It answered its own question: "No."

Finally, in a sort of stern postscript, the brochure added that the club members should not focus on the decorative aspects of the holiday, nor on the exchange of presents, but on their own personal, spiritual, and ideological quests. To aid in that regard, when they joined the club, each member would be given a small sapling to care for, the price of which was included in the initiation fee. In later years, the postscript explained, the member would watch the sapling grow and prosper along with her, right until the very day that both the member and her membership expired, at which time, the tree would be planted on top of the member's body (no embalming allowed) so, together, the two of them could go on expressing the lofty ideals of the Christmas Tree Club for decades to come.

Along with the tree, and included in the one-time initiation fee, each member also got a metal whistle, a membership card, and a loden-cloth forest keeper's hat.

Benefits notwithstanding, on that particular afternoon there were not many members in attendance, but why was not exactly clear to me. I guessed that one explanation for the lack of attendees (an addendum to the brochure described it as a "failure of the will") might have been the gradual substitution of lower-cost cremation for ground burial in the public agenda for the afterlife. Perhaps even more telling, however, was what the club's president (quoted in a card stuffed inside the brochure), called "the me-first/instant-gratification mentality of the unwashed socialist hoards in the pitiful decades that followed the great struggle." On the other hand, the reason may have been far simpler: what with people changing apartments, even homes, every couple of years, lugging around a living Christmas tree might just have been too much trouble.

I looked around the room for the fourth or fifth time, and as I did, a blonde woman wearing a neat brown skirt and a blouse of loden green, her hair pulled into a tight bun, appeared from behind a curtain. She stamped the floor once with a sturdy hiking boot and called for silence.

"Welcome," she said. "As your club's president, today I have come with some good news and also some bad. Now, I will give you the bad news and will not mince words. Today, I am sorry to say, our featured speaker, Doorperson Muriel

Collins, of the Fellowship of the Open Door, is unable to attend our meeting to speak on her topic, 'Continued Lebensraum after Death.' Doorperson Muriel, they tell me, has had a somewhat severe accident, and although she is in the process of recovery, her doctors have ordered her not to accept any speaking engagements for the next several weeks. As sisters of the Axis of Women's Clubs, we extend our best wishes, and are looking to reschedule at a later date."

The club president clicked her heels and paused to allow a murmur of sympathy to ripple through the audience.

"Now the good news: Not long ago I attended a meeting of the Ladies of the Rising Sun, another member of our Axis of Women's Clubs, where I enjoyed the sight of a martial arts competition between a half dozen young men using as their weapons the kendo, or traditional Japanese long sword, and another six using nunchucks, or traditional martial arts thingamajigs. It was touch and go for nearly an hour, and at last the fight came down to only two warriors, one for each type weapon. Each of the young men was perspiring heavily, his nearly hairless chest gleaming with sweat, his nipples small and firm, the veins of his arms pumping with each heartbeat, little flecks of dry white spit beginning to form in the corners of his wide mouth. As I watched, from behind me I could hear the heavy breathing of a woman who, I think, might never have seen such a sight before, and when I turned to ask her to keep the noise down what should I see but a woman who was wearing a shirt of loden green and a matching forest keeper's hat.

"When the competition was finally decided in favor of the nicely built boy who had been using the sword, I introduced myself to her, and you can imagine my delight when I found I was speaking to none other than Frau Elise, the president of the Christmas Tree Club of Munich, Germany, one of the original branches, so to speak, of our tree." She put out her arms to indicate the branches of a tree and several members of the audience clapped. "Why she came here without first telling us of her visit to Cleveland is a story that I will save for another time, I think. So without much more ado, let me present to you my good news, president of the Munich Christmas Tree Club, our speaker today: Frau Elise."

A round of enthusiastic applause followed as, from the right side of the stage area, a severe-looking woman of middle age walked up to the podium and looked out at us. I remember thinking that the last time I saw stockings with seams up their backs was in a black-and-white movie. "Hail American sisters of our original Christmas Tree Club," she said and snapped her arm straight out from her side in a smart rendition of a branch from a Christmas tree. Whether spouses were permitted to sit in on meetings of the German version of the club or not, I didn't know, but Frau Elise ignored my presence.

"Greetings I bring you from across the ocean, from your 'mutter' club, so to speak, and from the land of the original Christmas tree, by which I mean of course the Schwartz-wald, or famous Black Forest of Germany, where lives the Tannenbaum, the pure German spruce. Accept no substitutes. Ha, ha. I make a joke. Everywhere in America I hear of people using for Christmas trees Scotch pine, Douglas fir, arborvitae, Austrian pine, Black Hills spruce, eastern white pine, blue spruce, Fraser fir, and white spruce. Now where,

I ask you, will it stop? At oak trees? At stinky eucalyptus or sappy maples? Why there? Why not bushes, azaleas, or oleanders? Why not Christmas tulips? Why not Christmas roses, baby's breath, snapdragons, or maybe you Americans want sagebrush or Christmas tumbleweed? And what would you say *jew*-niper berries? This is one more joke I am making; do not be nervous. Because you know there is only one pure tree, and that is der Tannenbaum."

Frau Elsie was breathing heavily. "And now I am back to more serious Frau Elise again, so I am warning you, but I hope nice: You are already mongrel race. I know this, though you try to be not; but unless you as a nation return to Tannenbaum, there will be big trouble in your future, not for you personally—you are good club members, I know this, do not get me wrong—but for your entire country, I promise."

I turned to see if somehow, as impossible as it might have been in such a small and now increasingly uncomfortable space a latecomer might have entered without my noticing. I took a deep breath, and I don't know what caused it exactly—maybe the lack of circulation in the small, over-heated bunker and having to breathe in all those air fresheners at the same time, maybe the words of Frau Elise herself—but I felt extremely dizzy. At any second I was going to vomit.

Quickly I rose from my seat and raced toward the door.

Outside, I sat on the curb for a good five minutes with my head between my knees and, when I looked up, there was the elderly gentleman his trench coat. "Are you all right, son?" he asked.

"I'm OK," I said. "I just got dizzy in there for a minute."

He nodded knowingly. "That Christmas Tree group is a bad lot, if you ask me." He sighed and headed off in search, I guess, of strangers.

Around me was the usual rubble: the bent traffic signs, the pieces of concrete with iron rods sticking out, and, tacked to a phone pole, an assortment of posters advertising weight-loss plans and lost pets. I stood up and leaned against the telephone pole as I breathed in deeply. It was a struggle to regain my physical and mental equilibrium. Clearly there was a more sinister side to Cleveland than I had ever guessed from my comfortable apartment above Love Hurts. I shut my eyes and opened them. Was it possible that my own mother had once been a member of this so-called club?

Suddenly I felt another wave of nausea. For there, right at my eye level, tacked to the pole by something that resembled a miniature bowling pin, its head cream-colored with a red stripe around its neck, was a photo: small, square, yellowed, creased, dog-eared, and grimy. The picture was of me, still a baby, wrapped in a baby blanket and reaching toward a pile of whiskered, dead catfish heaped onto a wooden picnic table, being watched over by my oh-so-much younger mother.

13

IT WAS ABOUT A WEEK
after the meeting of the Christmas Tree Club, a Thursday,
I think, or possibly the following Friday afternoon. I was
talking on the phone with Marty about yet another wave
of murders, this time spread over a wide geographical area
and committed with a certain brand of pruning shears my
company specialized in distributing (what was happening
in people's gardens?), when I heard the sound of a powerful
motorcycle engine outside my window. A silence followed,
which was then broken by the sound of two heavy boots
bounding up the stairs, followed by a rapid knocking on my
front door. I opened it. It was Uleene, all right; the veins in
her forehead were throbbing, and the dog-eating-its-own-
intestines tattoo was pulsing with agitation.

"Uleene," I said, "what's wrong?"

"Ted," she panted, "they found Sarge."

"Well, good. Is he all right?"

"Far from it." Uleene's face twisted horribly.

"What happened?" I asked. "Can you tell me?"

Uleene pointed to a chair as if she were asking permission to sit down. I nodded and brought her a pillow to put under her; that particular chair, I knew, was old and could be uncomfortable.

"They finally got around to running a couple of grappling hooks back and forth through the middle of Aurora Pond," she said. "Can you guess what they found?"

"Sarge?"

"Yes," Uleene gulped. "He'd been shot six times by a .22 at close range, then tied to a concrete anchor by about ten yards of six-pound test clear monofilament."

"Poor Sarge," I said. "Was it a mob hit or something like that? But I'm glad they finally found him."

"I don't think it was a mob hit," Uleene said, and she got another strange look on her face.

"So who did it?" In truth I was beginning to find Uleene's fidgeting, plus her weird facial expressions, to say nothing of her unannounced appearances and disappearances, a little annoying. I knew she was trying to be helpful, but the chair she was sitting in was starting to squeak. If it broke they would probably take it out of my security deposit.

There was a long pause. Then Uleene resumed.

"You should know," she said, "that a half-used roll of six-pound test clear monofilament was found earlier in your mother's tackle box."

"I don't see what's wrong with that," I said. "Everybody knows that six-pound test clear monofilament is, if not the most popular choice for freshwater fishing, then certainly one of the top ten."

Uleene brightened momentarily but then looked downcast once again. "The other problem is that the police have just revealed there was also a .22 pistol in your mom's tackle box, and it had been fired recently."

"Wait a minute, are you trying to tell me that two or three months after her death my mother may have shot Sarge?" I asked.

"Of course not," Uleene answered. "At least, I don't think so. But the police seem confused. They just finished questioning me, and they say that your mom's their prime suspect. But being that she's—as you already said—officially dead, they're not sure how to proceed. To top it off, they sprinkled some kind of black powder all over El Diablo. They claimed it would turn up any incriminating fingerprints. I don't think they found any, but it's made a real mess. I told them your mom was innocent, but that didn't seem to slow them down. Now they're looking for her. If she *is* alive, Ted, we have to find her before they do. If she's alive, she just *has* to be at a meeting at some club or another, but I think we're starting to run out of venues. I gather she wasn't at the Christmas Tree Club?"

"That place," I said. "Why didn't you warn me?"

"If I had, you might not have gone," she said. "Anyway, I told you it wasn't to everyone's liking. You didn't by any chance see a heavy-set woman with short blonde hair and a ring through her right eyebrow, did you? Her name would have been Gretel."

I said that she'd said hello.

Uleene groaned but she looked pleased. She pushed herself up from the chair, and then sat back down with a helpless slouch. "If your mom's around we've got to find her before the police. I don't suppose *you* have any ideas, do you?"

"Only one, and it's a long shot," I said. I walked into the kitchen to the cabinet where I had put the picture of my mother and me that I'd found stuck to the telephone pole. "Can you make anything of this? I found it on a pole outside the Christmas Tree Club. That's me, as a baby, by the way." I held out the picture with the tiny bowling pin still attached to the top. To my surprise, Uleene completely ignored the picture, handing it back to me without even taking a look or exclaiming how I had changed, but held on to the pin.

"Holy smoke!" Uleene said. "I'd completely forgotten about the All City Bowling League. They meet at noon on the third Saturday of every month at a place called the Rainbow Lanes."

I must have looked puzzled because Uleene continued. "The All City Bowling League . . ." she said, and I could hear the edges of her voice trying to take refuge from the trying present-tense situation by snuggling between the fabric-softened sheets of the past. Her voice drifted to another spot. "When I was a baby, my mother used to slip me into an extra bowling bag and take me along as she rolled gutter ball after gutter ball with her friends. Mother always was a lousy bowler, but she sure loved the All City Bowling League. 'It's not about knocking down pins, Uleene,' she used to say. 'Anyone can do that, dear. It's about the sounds, the friends, getting into the groove, and then falling out of the groove.' Even later, after she had her stroke, she used to roll her wheelchair down to the Rainbow Lanes, find an empty lane, let drop a ball, and just watch it set there. You know, Ted, I have a good feeling about this. Believe me, there's something about the Rainbow Lanes that's special. I think that if there's anywhere you'll find your mother, it's there."

"I'm sorry that your mother had a stroke," I said. "I didn't know."

"That was nothing compared to what followed," Uleene said. She got up and started to pace around the room. I could tell she was thinking.

"Hey," she said, "maybe *your* mother had some kind of stroke. Maybe a stroke could be her defense for shooting Sarge. I'm here to tell you people can do strange things when they're not feeling their best. Of course, I'm not saying your mother did it."

"Of course she didn't," I said. "When does this All City Bowling League meet next? How far into the month are we?"

Uleene and I walked into the kitchen and looked at the Love Hurts calendar on the refrigerator. I'd gotten it as a housewarming gift from Raul when I moved in. Suddenly, I was embarrassed by the scenes depicted above each month; as luck would have it, September was one of the worst. Uleene shrugged as if she saw that sort of thing every day. "Forget those pervs," she said, using her finger to count off the squares. "It looks like we have twelve days until the twentieth. Let's hope the police don't get lucky before we do."

"Right," I said. "But can you think of anything I can do between now and then to help my mother? I know it's tough on you with Sarge murdered and all, but now that you've told me about what I guess I'd call your prior relationship you must be able to offer some piece of advice, no matter how small."

Uleene opened the refrigerator and took a couple gulps of milk straight out of the carton. She wiped her mouth with a dish towel. "I wish I could, sugar," she answered, "but I don't think there's a lot anyone can do at this point. I'll keep my eyes open, naturally, but until the bowling league meets, all we can do is pray that the police don't spot your mom before we do. According to my horoscope, these next couple of weeks are critical. That is, if your mother isn't dead."

She walked into the next room and over to the front window, where she took a long look down at the street. "The coast is clear," she said. "I was afraid I might have been followed. Meanwhile, it would probably be a good idea if we weren't seen together for a while. But don't worry," Uleene said. "The All City Bowling League is money in the bank. I've got a good feeling about this one. Trust me."

tape seven

INTERVIEWER: And they call you?

GUEST: The Old Trapper.

INTERVIEWER: That's an interesting name, Old Trapper. Is there a story that goes along with it?

GUEST: [unintelligible]

INTERVIEWER: Well, your outfit is for certain one we don't get to see every day, at least not here in our studios in the big city. All those skins and things . . . what do you call them, anyway?

GUEST: Pelts. I call them pelts.

INTERVIEWER: So, I'm guessing that must be how you got your name, in a way—wearing all those skins and pelts and whatnot wherever you go.

GUEST: That's part of it, sure, but the main part is me knowing that each one of these things I'm wearing was caught personally by me, so each item represents a little story all in itself, except, of course, for the wristwatch, which I bought at a discount jewelers. The watchband, though, that's my work. It's actual skink leather tanned by yours truly, not something you'll find in the stores, if I'm not mistaken.

INTERVIEWER: Yes, it certainly is remarkable, I'll say, as is your entire outfit and your story.

GUEST: Thanks. I love my outfit. I already told you that every part of my wardrobe has a kind of history—the tale—that's T-A-L-E—of some small or not-so-small animal caught in a trap, often screaming in terror as it sees me approaching, carrying the heavy cudgel I use to club them senseless so as not to spoil the pelt. I can't express the satisfying feeling it gives me to be wearing these same animals now as clothes, all of which I stitched myself, by the way. For what it's worth, I was going to bring the cudgel to the show this morning, but it kind of makes people nervous so I left it at home.

INTERVIEWER: I see. And your story about falling through the ice and seeing the tunnel?

GUEST: What about it?

INTERVIEWER: I was hoping you could describe that experience to our listeners.

GUEST: There's not that much to tell. I was walking across the lake—you know, taking a short cut to a couple of traps I had working on the other side—and the ice broke so I fell in and thought I was a goner, until I saw the tunnel, you know, part of an abandoned beaver lodge, so I could see a little light surrounded by a whole lot of roots that I used to pull me up and out of the water. Then I built a fire and dried myself off. The amazing thing was that I never even caught a cold afterward.

INTERVIEWER: A fire?

GUEST: Yes, I always make sure I've got a butane lighter with me. They light even when wet.

INTERVIEWER: So you were spared.

GUEST: Well I didn't get a cold, if that's what you mean, Bernard. As for the spared part, I would have to say that's a relative term. Who are really spared are all these animals I'm wearing. They'll be around—at least their skins will—longer than you or me. Even your shoes, Bernard, look at them—and they seem to be good ones—don't forget they were animals once. What do you want to bet they'll be turning up in an estate sale one day, if you get my drift?

INTERVIEWER: So you're saying that surviving in any form at all is the important thing?

GUEST: Well, sure I am. I don't want to go into a lot of scientific detail at this point about the latest developments in DNA research and human cloning at this time, but you probably know as well as I do the general direction they are all heading. What I'm saying is that survivors can't be picky—and that means me and you.

INTERVIEWER: Yes . . . but . . . I mean . . . are you telling me that my shoes . . .?

GUEST: Yes, Bernard. That's exactly what I'm saying.

14

OF ALL THE TIME I'D
passed in the city of Cleveland, the days I spent waiting for
the next meeting of the All City Bowling League were the
hardest, given the suspicion that Sarge's death seemed to be
casting on my mother's name. I took walks. I ate donuts and
put on a few more pounds. I worked on a new sculpture. I
took a bus out to Lake Erie, where I saw many dead perch. I
took the bus back.

Then Sunshine disappeared. I stopped by her studio
one afternoon, ready to begin the second session of classes
I'd paid for in advance, and there was a For Lease sign in
the window. I looked inside. The familiar floor covering
of marble dust, wood chips, and dried EZ Sculpt had been
swept clean. My sculpture of Hera was also gone—to where
was anyone's guess. To make matters worse, according to
Marty, the gardening implement business was in a nation-

wide slump. An article in the *Plain Dealer* had the headline "Woman Batters Pit Bull with Weed Claw" but from the sketchy details the reporter had provided, I couldn't tell the brand. If it *was* one of our products I had hope that people might begin to think of them in terms of personal protection, but Marty said that a senator from an industrial state had recently introduced legislation that, if passed, would hold anyone who made or sold a gardening implement used in the commission of a crime liable. We were losing money hand over fist, Marty said, and the bank account was nearly empty, but at the same time he told me it wouldn't help matters for me to return immediately. "Don't panic," he said. "Things have to get better."

I still had my sculpting, at least for the time being, but I knew I couldn't spend every minute working on the new one or I'd get stale. I took a daylong workshop in decoupage, another in collage, and one in which we chose our favorite plant and food and color and then wrote a story about a character having a lonely meal in a health-food restaurant that included all these elements.

I was getting desperate. Then, on the afternoon before the very day the All City Bowling League was to meet, I was rummaging through the snack food section of Love Hurts—it was a lot easier than going to the convenience store three blocks away—when Raul walked up behind me.

"Hey, Ted," he said. "I never got a chance to thank you properly for filling in while little Theodora was being born. I've got a couple tickets to an Indians game after work tonight—want to come along? No pressure. I've talked about it with Janice, and it's OK by her. She says she'd rather stay home with the kid."

I turned it over for about a minute. As remarkable as it might seem, the whole time I'd been living in Cleveland, although I was sure that I'd walked past dozens of televisions with baseball games being played across their screens, I'd never actually watched the famed Indians perform in person at their current venue, Progressive Field. On the one hand, frankly, I had no interest at all in watching grown men throw a ball back and forth and every so often hit it with a stick (those poor rats!), but on the other I *was* feeling jittery with anticipation at the prospect of the bowling league the next day.

"Sure," I said. "What time?"

"See you at six," Raul said. "It's a night game and we can have hot dogs at the park—it'll be my treat." He rang up my three packages of Ritz Crackers with peanut butter filling and then turned to a worried-looking gentleman who was buying a collar with metal spikes and a matching leash.

"Don't worry," Raul told him. "It's you."

Around three, I left my apartment to attend the final session of my macramé workshop, but the fact is that after a person has worked with a material as substantial as artificial stone, tying a few loops in a piece of string seems trivial. I executed a few halfhearted knots and then gave my pillow cover to a large lady in a blue dress, who seemed happy to have it. "You finish," I said, and left. For the next two hours I spent my time looking at the ducks outside my window. They would soon be flying south for winter; if things didn't work out for them, they were ready to move on. Did a duck ever regret leaving its last pond behind? Did a duck ever change his mind?

At 6:00 PM sharp I heard a honk. Raul was waiting out front in an aqua-colored Ford Escort. He drove us to Progressive Field, where, after parking the car, he showed our tickets, found our seats, and helped me settle in. I'm ashamed to admit that through the first few innings of the Cleveland Indians game I was so preoccupied with thinking about the All City Bowling League the next day that I did little more than stare at the logo of the Indian team itself—a disembodied head with one single feather, probably a turkey's, emerging from behind it. I supposed the head was meant to depict one of the original Indians who used to inhabit the Great Lakes region before they were hunted down and killed by Europeans and their civilization-born diseases, but this particular logo/cranium—speaking as a recent arrival to the world of sculptural heads—puzzled me, and I decided the source of its peculiarity was its expression, an oversized grin made up, interestingly, of only one row of teeth. Whether they were uppers or lowers was impossible to tell.

Moreover, the Indian's teeth seemed to be not actually human or even mammalian because, as everyone knows, a mammal's teeth are arranged symmetrically on both sides of the mouth, to the left and to the right in either direction from the space in the middle. But this baseball-supporting Indian's teeth had no middle space. They began with one giant incisor jutting out directly beneath his large nose, smack in the center of his face, and then the rest of his teeth were clustered on either side. Possibly because of this bizarre dentition, I couldn't tell if the logo-Indian's grin was one of anticipation, apprehension, or merely heightened avarice.

Nor was the rest of the Indian's floating head helpful. His eyes, for example, looked to the left, the side most often associated with the demonic, but the actual object of his gaze was impossible to determine. In addition, his headband, which must have been applied at birth in a primitive skull-shaping process, was—by the time the artist had gotten around to drawing him—so tight that it actually caused the skin where his eyebrows should have been (for some reason he had no eyebrows) to be pulled up. Clearly the effect of such a stricture on any cranium could only be a corresponding diminishment in brain capacity. Whatever else might be said for his skull, there could not possibly be room for an ounce of intelligence inside. So what kind of Indian was this anyway?

Obviously (to me at least), the head that the baseball team had chosen for its logo was not the head of a chief, but that of the lowest Indian foot soldier, or maybe not even an Indian, but only an old Italian wearing a feather (there was a certain Mediterranean cast to its features), or a texture-coat house-paint salesman, or a shoemaker, or a bookie, but in any case, he was apparently a survivor, some complete imbecile who had managed to outlast all the more handsome and intelligent others of whatever race he was supposed to represent through his manic goodwill alone. "Theodore," the head seemed to be saying, "relax and enjoy the game; tomorrow when you attend the meeting of the All City Bowling League, all your questions will be answered."

I took his advice, and when I began to watch the game in earnest, the Indians were ahead three to one. Someone hit a ball. Someone else caught it. We cheered. Raul left his seat briefly, then returned carrying two hot dogs with everything on them and a pair of Diet Cokes. "For you," Raul said, handing me a drink and a mustard-slathered frankfurter. "This is the life, huh?"

I began to relax a little more.

As a group of individuals, I had to say, the actual Indians team seemed remarkably carefree and good-spirited. The evening was warm. The lights on the field attracted swarms of huge moths. Their wings were lit from beneath and, flickering, they made a beautiful gray—with flecks of blue and brown—cloud in the night sky above the ballpark. I sat looking upward, enjoying the feeling that I was in a tropical forest of orchids, my eyes rebounding from the Indian logo, to the team itself, to the canopy of moths, then back to the logo, the team, and the moths again, like an endless triple play. I was just beginning to settle into this pleasurable rhythm when a chill came over me that was not attributable to any breeze from off the lake. I was absolutely certain I was being watched.

I turned so quickly that in the process I dropped some mustard from the hot dog onto my lap, but I could see no one who might have been staring at me because the rapid transition from the stadium's bright lights to the shadowed faces of the crowd made it difficult to make out much of anything at all. I was beginning to wonder if I should make an appointment with an optometrist or if this sort of handicap was just one more of the indignities of approaching middle age.

And yet in that mysterious way we can often sense the gaze of another, even through a crowd or from behind us, I could feel a pair of eyes watching my back. Then, from somewhere over the murmur of the crowd I thought I heard someone calling out my name, "Ted, Ted Bellefontaine," and it was not my mother's authoritative contralto, but the voice of a man.

I turned again, and saw nothing.

Still, *something* was going on, so I pretended to look out on the field, but all the while kept my eyes shut, as I heard the other team (As? Astros? Angels?) tie it up. When I opened my eyes and whirled around a second time, I spotted above me, maybe twenty rows back, a man wearing a heavy brown overcoat that was much too warm-looking for this weather. On the seat to his left rested a large, dark bag, dripping as if he had brought a sack of snow cones, or maybe a half watermelon on ice to the game, because every so often a drop would fall from the seat to the stadium steps, where it would make a splash that was too far away to hear.

I stared at him and he stared back at me. Then, without saying a single word he slowly raised an arm in front of him, pointed it in my direction, and smiled. His hand was covered by a black glove, but was this a gesture of taunting disrespect, or of welcome? I couldn't tell.

I grabbed at Raul, who was worrying a stubborn peanut with his teeth. "Look over there!" I shouted. "Do you see that man?"

Raul turned and squinted into the crowd. "What man?" he said. "I can't see anything because of the lights."

I attempted to describe the man to Raul, but when I turned back to look at him either the lights had gotten to my eyes or the man had simply disappeared like half of an arcane mathematical formula. Then, as if the stranger's gesture had flipped the switch on some motor deep inside me, I was filled with an overwhelming urge to get up and walk around.

"Excuse, me," I told Raul. "I'm going to see if I can get some of the mustard off my clothes. I'll be back in a minute."

Raul shrugged, and I hurried off to find a restroom. When at last I found one (the signage was somewhat tricky), I stood before the tastefully designed washbasin and considered what had happened: in mere moments I had gone from being full of the spirit of feeling one of many, a part of a crowd, *e pluribus unum*, an Indians fan, a member of a fellowship I never knew I craved, to suddenly being completely drained—and all from the sight of that curiously chilly stranger. Could this possibly have been the same man my mother had seen outside her window before she disappeared? If so, no wonder she had called me up that night, upset and needing to talk. And back then what had I done to help her? How much comfort had I provided my own mother when she really needed some? I didn't want to think about it.

I stood before the sink, squirted a little scented soap onto one of the hand towels stacked beside it, and applied it to my pants. In front of me a message either ordered or advised—I couldn't be sure—"Protect your health and the health of others: Wash your hands."

"The health of others" I could easily understand, but how could washing my own hands after touching my own body possibly protect me? It didn't make sense and, worse, the false self-interest offered by the first half of the statement seemed to cast doubt on the more altruistic principles of the second part. Who did they think they were fooling? The health of others indeed—what could that possibly mean to a person whose mental health was possibly at risk?

I looked up for a moment to see if any mustard was stuck to the corners of my mouth, and an amazing thing happened: for just the space of a heartbeat, for the length of a hiccough, I could see nothing at all in the mirror but that stupid hand-washing notice—black letters in Optima Bold on yellow paper. Then once again my face was there, with no sign at all of mustard. What had happened certainly could be explained easily enough: some bubble in the brain or, more likely, the same sort of fumble in an optic nerve that is responsible for the phenomenon of déjà vu, where the viewer is under the impression he has seen the sight earlier because he actually has; it is just that the first time around his brain failed to process the image. I knew this was probably the case, but in reverse now, the me-less mirror I'd seen as I walked in now coming back to me. Only this time it was frightening because for that moment, however brief, I was not really there. For one heartbeat I did not exist.

I promised myself that right after the bowling league business was settled I would see an optometrist for sure, whether in Cleveland or in St. Nils didn't matter, as long as it was soon.

I dried my hands and walked back toward Raul, taking care to look for the stranger, who was, not surprisingly, nowhere to be seen.

By the time I found my seat the game was in the last half of the final inning with the Indians behind by one run. Between pitches I continued to search the crowd for another glimpse of the stranger, but saw no one who even came close to resembling him. Finally, amid a series of strikes and foul balls, the Indians went down in defeat. Raul and I exited. I scanned the faces of my fellow patrons for the one that belonged to that peculiar, disturbing man. He had vanished.

Raul and I drove back to Love Hurts in silence.

"So, Ted—I'm glad you could come along," Raul said, when we had pulled up to the curb in front of the store. "You seem to be a little upset after the game, but take it from me, you shouldn't worry. With such a great ball club as the Indians, you don't have to fret about the outcome of any particular contest; it's enough just to see them play their hearts out. And now, if you'll excuse me, there's a video that's supposed to be a good one I promised Janice I'd bring home from the shop, so I'll say good night." He disappeared inside Love Hurts, still open and still doing a brisk business at that hour.

I walked up to my apartment and picked out a suitable pair of slacks and shirt for my visit to the All City Bowling League the next day. I laid them across a chair; then I undressed and immediately fell to sleep.

I did not dream.

15

WHEN I WOKE, the first thing I did was make myself a pot of coffee. When it was ready, I drank all of it, along with five or six of those raised-dough donuts, to give me the energy I would need. Either way, success or failure, it was going to be a big day. I took an extra-long shower. I brushed my teeth twice. Was I stalling for some reason? Possibly, because whether I was to meet my mother that day or not, both prospects seemed equally upsetting. I stared at the mound of EZ Sculpt that was just beginning to take shape in my living room. It was starting to look a little like Venus, and I wished Sunshine were still around to offer her advice.

I got on a bus and then on another until I was standing in front of the Rainbow Lanes themselves, a huge, one-story building covered with pink stucco that had shiny pieces of metal pushed into it so it glinted in the sun. Impressive as it was, it was only after I walked though the heavy front doors of multicolored glass that I understood for the first time that to be a bowler in Cleveland was entirely different than being a bowler anywhere else in the world.

To begin with, there were not just five, or ten, or even twenty sparkling bird's-eye maple lanes to roll one's ball upon but—according to the brochure I took from a rack by the door—a full five hundred, at least half of them at that moment reverberating with the noise of heavy balls passing down and back again (via the automatic ball returns), each single rumble therefore multiplied by two hundred fifty, and joining the sounds of struck pins crashing and falling and being reset by automatic pinsetters, and then (Oh, "City of Loud Noises"!) added to this roar, like the intermittent snarls of a prowling tiger in a jungle at night, were the announcements of an overhead public-address system directing bowlers to any lanes that might soon be available for play.

Now add to that the beams of slowly moving colored lights shooting from the control box (the source of the previous public-address announcements), a sort of a gondola suspended from the ceiling by four thick gold cables. Inside was the light operator, who paused from time to time to speak over the PA system and waved one hand to the people below, even as his other hand must surely have been spinning dials, flipping switches, and adjusting rheostats so that the lights shining out of the box, like beams from some psychedelic police helicopter, poured onto each lane below in ever more dizzying combinations, each colored beam pausing only long enough to be reflected momentarily on the shiny surface of its lane before it shifted to another lane, itself replaced by another beam, and then another, and so on in a seemingly random and yet clearly guided-by-genius pattern such as I had never seen in my entire life. It was a lot to take in on a Saturday afternoon.

Also, speaking of sensory overload in general and good taste in particular, in place of the usual greasy burgers and fries I associated with those few bowling alleys I had visited in my past, the Rainbow Lanes possessed at least a dozen separate cafés within my field of vision, limited as it was by stacks of generic and ready-to-be engraved bowling trophies, bowling bags and bowling coffee mugs, bowling jackets and bowling sweatshirts with built-in thumb warmers. But even from my restricted view I could spot the cuisines of China, France, Mexico, Germany, Morocco, and Hungary—Iceland, as well—although there had to be dozens more tucked in distant corners, to say nothing of various types of snack bars, some of them entirely devoted to serving yogurt, while others specialized in cookies, corn dogs, various jerkies, or pizza. Not only that, but in a far departure from the paper plates and cups I remembered from my own unsophisticated past (Linda had been a member of a bowling league for a short while, and she'd had a brisk business selling kelp to other bowlers until she hurt her back and quit), if a bowler at the Rainbow Lanes ordered, say, a little coq au vin from the French café near lane 73, as soon as it was ready a waiter dressed in a beret and a horizontally striped T-shirt would walk on down to the lane where he or she was bowling and, speaking to the diner in a fake French accent, serve it on a tray with a warm baguette wrapped in a checkered cloth napkin on the side.

Now back to the sounds: Instead of the jukeboxes I remembered as the norm for the alleys where Linda had taken me, the Rainbow Lanes had at the very least three sets of strolling musicians—a jazz trio, a lone gypsy violinist, and a sizable mariachi band. It was this last group who, though they seemed to make their home base near the Mexican café at lane 237, would every so often, in a burst of Latin high spirits, suddenly rush out from their natural habitat to make a brief but thrilling sweep across all five hundred lanes before they returned.

I rented a pair of size-twelve, orange bowling shoes with white stripes. "Is this where the All City Bowling League meets?" I asked.

The man behind the counter shook his head in an appreciative way at the naïveté of my question. "Look around you, man—lanes 1 through 325." He waved his arms. "There, that's your All City section."

I followed his gesture to see a panorama of lanes set off from the rest by red, white, and blue crepe paper, the first sections of which were occupied by a group of women wearing the familiar choir robes and silk headscarves of the Fellowship of the Open Door. They favored, I noticed, bowling balls of a light iridescent blue, the blue of heaven, but though I searched for Doorperson Muriel among them I could not find her. Possibly, she was still out of action from her injuries.

I walked to where the rest of the league was busy playing and inhaled along the way the scents of garlic, Szechwan peppers, bowling chalk, perspiration, fine wine, spilled orange drink, perfume, and the sweet scent of foot sweat leaking out from what must have been thousands of leather bowling shoes. Just beyond the Fellowship of the Open Door were the sturdy green-shirted bowlers of the Christmas Tree Club, and beyond them, a half dozen tottering Rotary Lions, followed by a scattering of Hot Clubbers—among them Raul's wife, Janice, wearing a filmy pink bowling shirt, trying to get back her prebaby figure, I supposed. Each threw a ball of what I guessed was her favorite color and watched as it rolled, fast or slow, according to her technique, down the alley to the little shivering grove of pins at the far end. And those were just the women's clubs; in the men's section were Moose, Elk, Lions, Eagles, Optimists, and also—surprisingly for Cleveland—Pessimists, who would roll their balls down an alley and then turn their backs without even looking to see what happened before they slumped back again, completely dejected, into their booths. In addition, there were whole sections for people with eating disorders, attention-deficit sufferers, recovering alcoholics, and practicing ones, too.

"Hey, Buddy," someone called from a knot of bowling grocery checkers. "We're short a member and will have to forfeit our match if you don't help us out. Want to give it a try?"

I said I would. I bowled an eighty-three, a seventy-one, and then, getting the hang of it, a ninety-six. It was more fun than I had expected. In between turns I kept an eye out for my mother, but saw nothing. It looked as if this was going to be another dead end, although a more pleasurable one than those women's clubs.

I lost track of all time, until hours later, when amid a chorus of oohs and aahs, trophies were handed out for the Best Team, Best Game, Best Series, Most Improved Player, and Worst Player. This last would have been me, except that a lady from the Rotary Lions argued that because I wasn't an official member of the All City League, I wasn't eligible. Still, they did give me a really nice souvenir penlight, run by two AA batteries. It was black and chrome, and inscribed on its side were the words "City of Strikes."

I checked my watch. It was late. The league was breaking up, and while some bowlers continued playing, others were removing their shoes and preparing to go home. A sort of tremendous sadness began to overtake me, as at the end of a perfect day, when it's time to say good-bye and get ready for bed. "Good-bye, Cleveland," I said beneath my breath. "So long, Mom. I did my best, but enough is enough. I guess it's time for this son of yours to head on back to the ordinary world of St. Nils."

I began to trudge toward the stand where I'd rented my shoes and at that exact moment the lights, except for a dim glow that came from the control booth above me, went completely out. Then, from the booth, through the fuzz of the inexpensive loudspeakers and multiplied by the echoes of the Rainbow Lanes itself, I heard a woman's voice, a familiar one. It was the same one I had last heard on the other end of my phone only a couple of months ago, telling me good night and not to worry. But now the voice was darker, more urgent, and more gruff.

"Attention bowlers"—the words reverberated through the cavernous space below it—"I am sorry to interrupt your afternoon of bowling pleasure, however for personal and safety reasons I have been forced to commandeer this booth and to make secure the pleasant gentleman who ordinarily runs it. His name, as some of you know, is Bob Hefferman, but do not worry; if none of you down there gives me any trouble (and you had better not), Bob will be released shortly, none the worse for wear."

In the dark I could hear a flurry of confusion among my fellow bowlers. Little by little the balls that had been rolling came to a halt. And then the voice continued. "Theodore Bellefontaine, I can see you down below although you obviously cannot see me. That part, however, is not important, but my message is, Theodore, and it's for you."

I waved a greeting vaguely in the direction of the booth while I tried to see the figure that was speaking. The voice was correct. I could see nothing.

"Mother?"

I sat down heavily in an empty vinyl-covered booth.

"Don't be a ninny, Ted," the voice resumed, and although I could not be absolutely sure the voice *was* my mother's, who else would speak to me like that?

"And as for the rest of you bowlers," she was saying, "you may as well know that this is a private conversation between a mother and her son. It doesn't concern you, though frankly I have no objection to your listening in. Who knows? It may prove educational."

I sat in the dark and thought about it: if this voice *did* belong to my mother, she seemed to have toughened up considerably even from the woman I knew in St. Nils. She sounded fierce and fearless. Maybe she *had* killed Sarge.

Maybe my own mother had somehow become a hardened criminal after death. Maybe that's what death did to a person.

The crowd, already hushed from the extinguishing of the lights, grew attentive. In the darkened alley around me I could make out the shapes of several bowlers sitting quietly, cradling their heavy balls in their laps.

"However"—my mother seemed to be on a roll—"for those of you who *are* out there listening, despite the fact that you probably only came here for an uncomplicated afternoon of bowling, I want you to know that you are about to hear, as a kind of bonus, the story of a mother's love, of a mom's passion and protection, and, at the same time, a tale of murder and this particular mom's staying one step ahead of the law, a story that is in many ways very like a Greek tragedy, though it will also differ substantially from that classic format in several of its major components."

Some fool clapped a couple of times, but except for that, you could have heard a pin drop.

"So, Ted," the voice from above went on, "there are a few things you probably don't know about my life, and I suppose now is as good a time as any to tell you. I apologize for this public venue, by the way, but circumstances being what they are, it's the best I can do. And as for those women's clubs I had you attend, my apologies; I *had* meant to meet you earlier at one of them, and sometimes I even got to the place I was supposed to be, but could only stay a minute or so before I lost whatever power I had and had to exit this world of the living in a hurry. This interfacing between realms is a lot more complicated than I thought at first. But suddenly several circumstances changed and . . ."

The sound system began to crackle and then whine, drowning out what my mother was saying. I didn't know whether it was a faulty transmitter or some sort of electrical problem that had to do with her materialization.

Then her voice was back again. "Anyway, Ted, the first thing you should know is that your mom is no plaster saint. I know it may have seemed unfair that I left when you were practically a baby, but who can compare the thankless work of raising a child with the spring of a lightweight fiberglass or composite rod as it whips to send a lure out thirty, forty, even fifty yards away and not vote for the latter? And that's not even to mention hearing the faint ping of a lure hitting the surface of the water, a small splash, then counting to five or more, depending on how deep you want it to sink before you start reeling in again, all the time feeling the pleasant pressure of the water as it resists, waiting for the jolt of a solid hit, the tug of Mother Nature. And yes, Ted, I said 'Mother Nature,' for she certainly would understand that there are more important things to do than to hang out with a kid as he watches his *The Best of Sesame Street* video for the six thousandth time. Mother Nature knows that there are forces in this world more important than life—or death, for that matter. God knows, I've never blamed Linda, she did her best, I know, but I do wish that woman had taken you fishing once or twice. Things might have turned out different."

It may have been my imagination, but I thought I heard murmurs of rising interest around me.

"In any case, as you may or may not know, it wasn't long after you were born that I left you in the caring hands of

Linda so I could become the common-law wife of a man who was both a sportsman and a lover. Unfortunately, it turned out, he was one of the most deeply selfish, most completely paradoxical individuals I have met: a protector of nature and nature's children, and yet, treacherously, also a friend to those who would desecrate it and steal her bounty."

I could guess what was coming.

"And you're right, Theodore. The man I speak of is Sarge," Mom said, "a man worth fighting for and reeling in, 'a keeper,' as they say, and, yes, finally—although they clearly will never take me alive—also a man worth shooting a half dozen holes into and deep-sixing into the tepid waters of Aurora Pond, though *not*, by the way, when he threatened to turn his hairy back on me—our relationship had been finished for years at that point, and I was keeping plenty busy with the transcription stuff—but when he broke his sacred promise, that, Ted, is when I made up my mind that I had to kill him."

I could hear my heart beat once, twice, then a third time. A couple bowlers, who must have been fishermen as well, said, "Sarge."

"Bear with me," my mother said. "From this point on things get a little complicated, but by the time I finish I'm sure you'll understand everything."

The crowd in the bowling alley groaned. I could hear what I supposed were maintenance people moving around with brooms and dustpans, but I didn't know how they could see well enough to clean anything.

"But, Ted, everybody, be patient. The truth, for all its complications, is simple enough," my mother said. "Ted, you were just a baby when I left you in the care of Linda. Your father was dead, and I was struggling to hold down a job as an artist's model, raise you, and also get in a little fishing on the side. I don't suppose you can understand this, but once a person has been bitten by the fishing bug, it's impossible to get rid of. Anyway, when I met Sarge, who had come to St. Nils for a fishing equipment convention, I fell for him hook, line, and well . . . you know. But Sarge said he wanted no part of a family, and meanwhile Linda said having a kid to raise would be a helpful cover for her line of business, so when she offered me the money to leave St. Nils for Cleveland to be with Sarge, I accepted. Then, soon after I arrived here, I became pregnant."

There was a startled squawk from the PA.

"I thought of aborting it, but didn't, and I don't know if it was from all the over-the-counter drugs that I'd taken for my morning sickness, or from some chemicals Sarge had inhaled in the war, but the baby didn't turn out so well. When I gave birth to your half brother—which happened to be in the exact same shack out of which Sarge sold bait—Sarge took one look at him and said, 'Helen, I don't know what your other son is like, but this kid of ours looks exactly like a slug. Can't we please just dump him somewhere so he'll become someone else's problem?'"

My half brother? Did I have a half brother? If so, what had become of him? The lights of the alley started to flicker, and I could see a couple bowlers check their watches. Then it went dark again, and my mother continued talking. "And, honestly, in the long run, who knows? As cruel as it sounds, Sarge may have been right; that might have been better, but

I was all full of those hormones, so of course I said no, that we should wait and see how your brother turned out. 'Don't worry,' I told him, 'things will improve,' and that seemed to settle him for a while—that and alcohol."

The crowd let out a resigned sigh as if they, or at least a large number of them, might have heard that "things will improve" line before.

"So Sarge and I lived together at the bait shack. Sarge spent more and more time out on the pond every day and was starting to drink pretty heavily. He kept Aurora Pond stocked with trout, trophy bass, catfish, and bluegills for the small fry, while I took care of your brother. In order to make ends meet, I took a job or two as a transcriber, an ideal at-home industry, and then it turned out I actually grew to like it. And your brother *did* improve, or at least he didn't get much worse—he became more human in many ways, though not exactly enough to do anything. In the end he was stuck between being a person and something else, though I can't be sure precisely where I'd put him on the evolutionary scale—I'm guessing maybe somewhere in the upper neighborhood of a fish, because he spends so much of his time in the water—or maybe not. But at least he's not mean, and he has the sweetest smile you'll ever see . . ."

"*Spends? Has? See?*" I said, and I could hear an uneasy stirring in the dark of the alley.

"Yes, *has*," Mother answered, "but I will get to that soon. Anyway, there we lived, the three of us, at the bait shack, while you were making a bundle back in St. Nils. Meanwhile, Sarge, no doubt from the twin pressures of wildlife management and being a father, kept drinking more and more. Then it turned out that, drunk or not, he couldn't keep his hands off other lady fishermen. The last straw was when he had an affair with some biker chick half his age who really didn't even like to fish but who had only come out to the pond to pass some time. That was when I finally left him, but only after he promised to take good care of your brother. Are you following this, Theodore?"

I nodded into the darkness, mindful of the fact that Sarge had refused to take care of *me* when *I* needed a dad. But then again, Sarge wasn't really anyone's dad at the moment. He was dead. I could hear a few people trying to explain things to others who were evidently confused.

"Anyway, Theodore—and anyone else who happens to be listening," my mother continued, "this brings me to the whole point of this awkward interruption of the All City Bowling League, and why I sent those cards asking you to come to Cleveland in the first place. When I sent you that first postcard I was already dead, of course, but I hoped that you might show up anyway and I could break through the life/death barrier long enough to arrange a talk between you and Sarge to make him hear reason, maybe even tell him how hard it had been for *you* to be abandoned. I wanted to give you more information, of course, but this writing messages from the grave isn't as easy as some people may think; most people don't realize that it takes over an hour even to write down one single letter, and days to complete an entire sentence. Also, for some reason I never could understand . . ."

The sound went off completely. There were sparks coming from the gondola and I worried about the danger of a fire, but no one else seemed very concerned. Then my mother finished saying something I couldn't quite make out about the Treasure Chest. "Now with Sarge gone, your brother has got to be starving, if he's even still alive," she concluded.

The voices of people explaining things were getting louder.

"Because you see, dear, what with the police stakeout and the house-to-house searches, I can't get within a mile of the pond myself, dead *or* alive. But *you*, nobody's after you. So it's up to you to go there and feed him—shiners or hellgrammites, or crawlers—he'll probably take anything because he's never been a picky eater. I need you to somehow make him understand that it's all right; that he's going to be OK, but from now on—or at least for a long while—he's going to have to get along by himself."

"Does my brother have a name?" I shouted up into the darkness. I caught a whiff of fresh baked bread from the French café.

Mother stopped for a long time, as if pondering. "That's a good question, Ted," she answered. "When he was first born he looked so strange, as I mentioned, it was impossible to decide what a creature like that, even if he *was* my own child, should be called, particularly because Sarge and I weren't even sure he was going to live. But he did live, and as he grew older, and we more or less got used to him, by that time it seemed silly—even superficial—to tack a name onto so elemental a being. Sarge, though, had a mean streak, which is what finally got him killed, and after he'd had a few brews he used to call his son Private Zero. So it came to be, in the absence of anything else, I more or less got used to thinking of him as that. But, technically, the answer to your question is no, he doesn't have an official name, nor does he have a birth certificate."

"You're positive he's a he, then?" I thought I smelled smoke coming from somewhere.

"Well, actually, I don't know that for certain. But Sarge, having been in the military and all, was in the habit of dealing with boys, so I thought, what the hell, why not? That way Sarge could have a son at least, and you could have a brother, even if you were unaware of his existence. In time Zero grew up to be a whatever, and mostly he learned to take care of himself, except for his meals. So back when Sarge was still alive, every evening after the fishermen had gone home, he would walk to the end of the dock and lower a bucket or two of fish heads and worms—sometimes, as a treat, some old cheese bait—into the water, and Zero would have supper. Once in a while, I guess during what you might call his adolescent period, Zero took to sulking, and we'd have to take a boat out to look for him with the fishfinder, but thank heaven that's passed. So to make a long story short, Sarge and Zero seemed to be doing well enough together that I thought I could visit with you in St. Nils. Then once I was there, I didn't feel bad about staying far longer than I'd planned. I figured it would do Sarge good to cool his heels, so to speak. And everything *was* fine until the evening the stranger stopped outside the Treasure Chest, and I realized I had to go back to Cleveland. But the good news is that the tunnel everybody talks about going through isn't one way, and I said to myself, Helen, if you could be dead while you were still among the living, then there's no reason you can't do it again. All you need is to go in the opposite direction. So I tried, and I failed, and it *was* harder than I thought it would be, but, as you can tell, I finally made it work."

I could hear a gasp of disbelief come from those listeners who were still following, and, frankly, I was surprised all over again myself.

"How?" I mouthed the word, and then I formulated the entire question that had been on my mind since my mother had first begun this conversation: "How is such a thing possible?"

There was another long pause, as if my mother were considering how much she could, or would, tell me and, by extension, our audience. Finally she spoke: "Ted, this whole process is very, *very* complicated—much too much for practically anyone, let alone a fun-loving sportswoman like me, to understand—but let me try to explain as best I can. The last time I saw you was right before I left for Cleveland, the city known as the 'Passage between Life and Death,' though it's not the only one, of course; sooner or later everyone who's about to die . . ." Whatever she said next was drowned out by the noise of the sound system's popping and screeching and the poofing of more sparks coming from the gondola. My mother rolled along as if she hadn't heard a thing because, possibly, for all I knew, she hadn't: " . . . and so it was only when I left St. Nils for here, the 'Best Location in the Nation,' that I could come to terms with being dead when I thought I wasn't."

My mother paused to let this sink in, just as I imagine it must have taken time for it to sink in the first time she thought about it.

"And, Ted," she continued, "I know you've heard about a mother's love crossing all boundaries and so on and so forth, haven't you? I admit that when it came to raising you I wasn't much of a mom, but basically—and you should take this as a compliment, Ted—you turned out a lot better than I would have guessed. Surely, though, you can understand that your brother is a different matter entirely. I'm worried about Zero, and despite the fact that Sarge gave me a big speech about how I shouldn't worry about Zero just before I went out in the boat to try to teach your brother how to catch his own fish, and then I slipped, hitting my head on the side, it was obvious that the man's mind was elsewhere. I guess you can see what I'm getting at, right?"

I heard murmurs of confusion from those bowlers still listening, while others were lighting up cigarettes as if they were resigned to waiting the whole thing out. A shower of sparks arced down from the gondola. I was getting even more worried, but I still seemed to be the only one.

My mother was going on. "It was only when I found out—and don't ask me how any of this works, Ted, because it's complicated and involves a fair amount of particle and other kinds of physics, too—that Sarge was planning to turn his back on a whole generation of sportsmen by handing Aurora Pond over to a consortium of real-estate developers who called themselves Aurora Shores, and in the process would be murdering his own son because he was well aware that these same developers planned to fill about two-thirds of the pond up with toxic landfill, that I finally got mad enough to go the extra mile to return and shoot the man. So now here I am today at the Rainbow Bowl, talking with you more or less in person once again."

I sank silently into a booth and felt a cold something creep into my body. Apparently I had settled down upon a dish of ice cream. Around me the crowd broke into shouts of "Shame" and "Hooray." They seemed about equally divided.

"So you'll do this for me, Ted?"

The crowd grew silent.

From behind me a lone mariachi begin to noodle quietly on his trumpet, but my mother ignored him.

"Ted, listen up. You need to tell Zero not to be afraid, to get him back into good eating habits, to explain the situation. A part of him is you, Ted, and you're all he has left. Private Zero needs you. You don't have to worry about the real estate thing, by the way. The whole deal fell apart when the developers heard that Sarge was killed. I think they're going to turn the pond into a nature conservancy or something."

I thought of my brother, hungry and alone, no doubt having been frightened by the yellow crime-scene tape, the irritating red lights of the police cruisers, and the annoying crackle of their walkie-talkies. It didn't seem as if it would be so terribly difficult to do what my mother was asking when I compared it to the round of often violent women's club meetings I'd completed, or compared to what she, as a lone mother—though not without her faults—had accomplished.

Go out to the pond; find whatever; feed Private Zero something; tell him not to worry. Let him know that it's time he took care of himself for a while—for a long while. Say bye-bye. Go back home to St. Nils. End of story. My mother had wanted to see me, not for my sake, but for my brother's. On the one hand, I felt like crying. On the other, I had to admit I was proud of her.

"Sure, Mom," I said. "No problem."

"Good," my mother said. "Now time's a-wasting, Theodore. You'd better get moving."

Then there was a small scuffing sound, amplified by the public-address system, and a fair-sized explosion and flames coming out from the gondola, followed by what must have been the hollow whoosh of a portable fire extinguisher, because the flames went out. The lights came back on. All around me bowlers picked up their balls and sent them hurling down the once-again brightly colored alleys. Above me, Bob Hefferman stuck his head out of the gondola and made a V for victory sign. These Clevelanders were a level-headed group, that was for sure.

What had just happened? I blinked in the light and walked back to the rental booth to return my shoes and get my deposit back.

Somebody behind me rolled a ball.

I exited the Rainbow Lanes into the outdoor sounds of cars, horns, and screeching brakes, which now seemed positively restful. The sun was going down and a cool breeze was blowing in from Lake Erie. I looked for a bus but saw nothing remotely like a bus in sight. How time had passed

tape eight

INTERVIEWER: So you are saying that . . .

GUEST: I'm saying that as we approach what I like to call the "death state," the walls that separate one memory from another, or even what happened twenty years ago from five minutes ago, break down, and we find ourselves in a sort of No Man's—or No Woman's—Land of Zero Time. Therefore, if all these memories are constantly interrupting where we are at the moment, they in effect push aside the present tense and replace it with the past, or in some cases, mistakenly though, with the future. So, Brad, it's as if we're living in a place where everyone has a watch, but you see, these watches are running at different speeds. And if that's true, then so much for those good old laws of physics regarding time and space that you and I were raised with. I hope I'm being clear.

INTERVIEWER: Very much so. But then tell me, Carlotta, why should an attractive person like yourself wear a watch at all when I'm sure there are any number of men who would be only too glad to tell you the time of day or night if you asked them?

GUEST: Brad, that's an excellent question. And I'm afraid I don't actually have a complete answer to that one at the moment, but I'll try. Maybe I wear a watch only to attempt to make me feel there's some measure of certainty somewhere that I can look to, to provide a sense of serenity gained by wearing a watch set at least to one time, even if that time's not a real one, in the same way that a member of a primitive tribe or a young child will wear a watch as decoration, whether the watch works or not—despite, or maybe because of, the fact that no one has taught them to read time. For example, I notice you are wearing a watch right now, Brad, and, as you were kind enough to point out, of course, so am I.

INTERVIEWER: But then—and you can stop me if I'm totally off base here, Carlotta—suppose the person in question, for one reason or another regarding the laws of physics, is missing a wrist on which to put this watch? What would you say happens then?

GUEST: Ah yes. Well, Brad, you must have taken your smart pill today, for that is another excellent question. [laughs] I can see you've done your homework. I suppose that if they have no wrist, as you say, then they will just have to find some other part of their body, possibly their forearm or biceps, or even an ankle or a thigh, providing, of course, they can find a band large enough and that the numerals on the watch face are large enough to read from that distance, especially, because for a person who is approaching that death-state I mentioned earlier, there are various vision changes that accompany this process. You know about pocket watches, of course, but I've also seen watches—maybe you have, too—that come with little pins so you can pin them to your chest, with the numbers upside down so if you look at your chest, you can read them even though they would look upside down to anyone else who happens to be looking at your chest, as you are looking at my chest right now, Brad, and though I find it flattering, I'm obliged to say that I also find it uncomfortable.

INTERVIEWER: Yes, I can see what you mean, Carlotta, but putting all that aside, and just to take it one step further, suppose there's no body there at all, and certainly no chest, such as yours, to take just one magnificent example, that you can pin a watch to. What then?

GUEST: [laughs] Why, Brad, then I suppose what we do is to invent a new body, or something. Or look at a clock on a wall.

16

SO, FRESH FROM THE
revelations (and what revelations they were!) of the Rainbow Lanes, I found myself directing my steps again to the south and east of the city of Cleveland toward that pond named after the dawn. And it was not because I was not tired (I was—that bowling had worked a lot of muscles I wasn't used to) or because I was so certain that Private Zero would die without my help (he'd made it on his own this far; could a couple more days hurt?). No, I had two other reasons: First, I was frightened of what my mother might do to me if she'd already come back from the other world to commit murder and then had returned again to make me promise to take care of my brother. Second, and possibly more important, it was true that I had heard my mother's stern words about Zero needing me, but the fact was, at that moment, it was me who desperately needed Zero. This

mother-coming-back-from-the-dead business had rattled me more than I cared to admit and, oddly, the result was that I felt more alone than ever. I needed to be near someone who was a part of me, or at least shared a mom with me. I needed a brother—however remote and strange he might be—that I could touch, if only to affirm my own existence. Honestly, I couldn't predict whether going to the pond—and therefore to my mother's grave (even if I'd just finished talking with her a few minutes earlier)—would help or not, but in the end, really, what other option did I have?

The evening was becoming dark and chilly, and I hadn't thought to bring enough money for a taxi. Even though the bowling itself had been on the house, all I had was the few dollars I'd gotten back as my deposit for the bowling shoes. That left only my thumb.

Strangely, in a city so full of friendly and helpful individuals as Cleveland, I found myself having some difficulty in obtaining a ride, although, to give people credit, those commuters who didn't have the time to stop for me often slowed their cars as they passed to yell out various suggestions on what I should be doing instead. It grew darker, and colder, too.

I didn't know exactly where I was, only that I was somewhere pretty far out in the suburbs at that point. I walked along the side of the road and traveled for what I guessed was almost an hour without seeing a single car. People, or at least some of them, got to bed early in Cleveland. For the first time since I'd arrived, I breathed in the flat smell of winter. The night grew quieter, and in the shrubbery on either side of the highway I could hear the scurrying of various small animals: opossums and raccoons and, I was certain, a few rats as well. From a hill or two behind me, I could hear excited yelps and howls as a pack of wild dogs, no doubt formerly pampered family pets who had been tossed out on the highway at some first so-called family emergency: a death, a little drug addiction, a case of Alzheimer's—and had been forced to transform themselves to vicious killers.

The pack came closer, then closer still. I looked around for some weapon to defend myself with; not only could I find none, but my arm was starting to throb from all that bowling.

It was, therefore, with considerable relief that I first heard and next saw what turned out to be a sputtering Volvo station wagon coming slowly up behind me with its headlights off. I waved to show I could use a ride and waited until it pulled to a complete stop. The back of the wagon was full of cardboard cartons stuffed with brochures, and as I entered the passenger's side, I was startled to find its driver was none other than Doorperson Muriel herself, her turban temporarily coiled around the headrest of her seat.

"You look slightly familiar," she said. "Do I know you from somewhere? Do you have a library card?"

I thought it best not to mention that I'd witnessed her unwilling participation in a couple brawls; except for a small scar on her chin, which looked as if it was going to be permanent, she looked almost fully recovered.

I shook my head. "I don't think so."

"In that case . . ." Doorperson Muriel put the car in gear and made a gesture as if she were about to unwrap the turban from the headrest in preparation for some esoteric lecture. Her efforts caused the car to swerve dangerously, however, and I was happy to see she quickly gave the idea up.

"I'm not a girl who usually picks up strange men," Doorperson Muriel continued, "because there's too much that can happen to a woman driving the roads alone at night, far from help, not a farmhouse in sight, even in as safe a place as the greater Cleveland area, with no one to hear your cries, no other drivers to stop and offer a hand. But I must confess there was something about the impression you made standing alone in the night like that, waving your arms, that made me say: Here is a man, yes, and full of all the smoldering sexuality and power that men are capable of imposing upon a woman, Muriel, but here also is a man who looks as if he is ready to go beyond that superficial display of overwhelming strength and domination. Here is a man, Muriel, I said, who has suffered more than his share of loneliness and frustration, a man who is ready to walk through the door from one life into a better one, a man ready to be reborn, so to speak."

I don't know what it was, but suddenly it seemed that her voice was sucking out every ounce of oxygen from inside the small station wagon. I went from feeling cold just a moment earlier, to being in need of fresh air. "Do you mind if I wind a window down just a crack?" I asked.

"Down a crack . . ." Doorperson Muriel murmured. She began humming as if she were contemplating the idea, when suddenly a wild dog that looked to be a golden retriever—it was nearly invisible in the absence of her headlights—loomed up for a split second before the slow-moving Volvo. Doorperson Muriel stepped hard on the brakes and the animal disappeared again into the darkness.

"I'd rather you didn't," she said. "Now where was I?"

"Reborn," I prompted despite myself.

Muriel touched her hand to my knee and the car swerved again. "I was saying that each of us is born once, of course, but if we wish, we can also be born again, hence the word *rebirth* to signify a repetition of a birth, and such a concept, if it were not possible, would surely not exist as a word, would it? No, of course it would not, and instead there would only be a meaningless noise or something else, possibly a hum, or not even that, maybe nothing at all, maybe just silence. 'But wait,' you say, 'not so fast. Just because the word *rebirth* exists, it doesn't mean the act itself is simple, or even reachable for the ordinary person.' But hold on, I answer: that's why we have, for example, the word *difficult*—because this being born a second time takes a lot more effort than most people realize. You can't just stand around and wait for it to happen. A person has to find the right door, a different door than they used the first time around, on birth number one, and then they have to grasp the knob firmly in their right hand if they're right-handed, or, if left-handed, their left, and then they have to turn it, to pull, or sometimes to push on this door that is the barrier to their enlightenment, creating what I like to call 'an open door,' though technically a door can be neither open nor closed because it's just a slab of wood or sometimes glass or metal. That's not exactly the way the process works, of course, but I'm trying to put it in a way I hope that even such an attractive brute as you would understand. Also, I have to add in all honesty, without me wanting to discourage you, that the odds are slim that most of your testosterone-laden kind will ever experience such a revelation. You, however, as I was saying, seem somehow to be different . . ."

I couldn't tell if it was my imagination, but I thought I heard a ringing in my ears, just beneath which I could hear the words: "It just so happens that I belong to an organization called the Fellowship of the Open Door, and just the other day the sisters were discussing whether, if one of us happened to find some intelligent and, dare I say, *trainable*, though no doubt spiritually naïve young man, in fact exactly the sort of person I believe you may be, although if you want to be technical about it I wouldn't say you are exactly young . . ."

My head was starting to throb.

In the side-view mirror I saw a pair of headlights come up out of the dark behind us. They appeared to be trailing the Volvo, and I could tell that Doorperson Muriel had also noticed them.

"Do you have a cell phone for emergencies?" I asked, even though I knew that for her to take her hands off the wheel as she drove would practically be a guarantee of a double suicide. But the throbbing was increasing, along with the ringing in my ears. I pushed aside rising feelings of aggression and hopelessness. I kept watching the lights of the mysterious car behind us in the side-view mirror.

"If only," she said, "the real emergencies of life could be solved as easily as carrying a cell phone." Muriel stared ahead into the night and kept driving. "But it's important that you know when I refer to the Fellowship of the Open Door that I'm speaking of one of the oldest and yet most recent organizations in all of history, a combination, like the universe itself, of rueful wisdom and eternal hope, of the acknowledgment of various serious mistakes as well as the belief that we can learn from them. In addition, we at the Fellowship of the Open Door have a mind-set that erases the hierarchical differences between men and women and even, to some extent, those between humans and animals, although I personally draw the line there. Also, as a sort of no-cost extra, as they say in infomercials, we throw in a philosophy that stresses the simultaneous permanence and impermanence of all things, as well as the need to help the environment and to heal this precious planet of ours that has been so wounded by the greed and lack of foresight by those talentless idiots currently running the country out of Washington DC—I hope you're not a Republican. When you speak of emergencies, it just makes me laugh: Ha, ha. Down a crack indeed. Ha, ha, ha." She began to hum once again.

For the very first time in my entire life I had an inexplicable urge to strike a person I hardly knew—a person, after all, who had done nothing to me whatsoever but offer me a ride when I needed one. I *was* confused, and the ringing in my ears doubled, tripled, and overtook the throbbing, though the throbbing was giving it a good run for its money. Was this some hidden genetic legacy from the father I had never met? I hoped not. I picked up an empty soft drink can from the floor and began to make it as small as possible.

How much longer could I contain myself? Then an even stranger question suddenly struck me with the force of a blow. When I had been looking at the side-view mirror earlier, had I seen only the lights of the car following us, or my own face as well? I wasn't sure. The fact was that I didn't ing tickets, as well as one citation for disturbing the peace. I'm afraid you are going to have to return with me to the station. As for your passenger," he touched the brim of his hat to me, "sir, I'd say you are lucky to be alive after driving with such an irresponsible individual such as this. Depending on where you're headed, I can either take you back to the station with this lady or, if you prefer, you can wait here for the tow truck I've called to bring her car back. Maybe the driver can drop you somewhere on the way."

"Thanks, I'm on my way to Aurora Pond," I said.

The policeman pulled the car keys from the ignition and pocketed them. "If that's what you want, sir, but you should know that there have been reports of wild dogs in the neighborhood. I'll tell you what: I'll take the keys, but leave the car door unlocked, so if they threaten you, you can sit inside." He walked over to the patrol car and reached into its trunk. "Here," he said, handing me a black and shapeless knitted garment with a blood stain, "take this sweater with you in case you get cold. I got it off a perp about a week ago. You can drop it back at the station when you're done. Tell them Jeff is saving it to plant for evidence."

"Don't worry about me, Jeff. I'll be fine," I said. I put the sweater on and immediately felt more comfortable.

Muriel gave me a look as if I'd let her down, but then she brightened. "Officer," she said, "I don't suppose that any harm could come to me driving back with a big strong, intelligent man like yourself, could it?"

"Why now that depends," the policeman said, and laughed. "Isn't the job of the police to protect people from themselves?"

17

AND THEN, GRADUALLY,
the sounds of the wild dogs faded as the pack turned away in
pursuit of an unfortunate cat, an escaped pet bunny, or even
a whole coop of chickens some mom and dad were raising
so they could show their children the miracle of birth plus,
as a bonus, have fresh eggs every morning. I sat inside the
station wagon and felt my body relax. I'd had mixed feelings watching Jeff lead Muriel off in handcuffs, pushing her
head down so she wouldn't bump it on the doorframe of the
police cruiser; the ringing in my ears had disappeared, but
she *had* given me a ride. Inside the Volvo, Muriel's turban
was still wrapped around its headrest, looking like some pal-
lid reptile in an exhibit at the zoo. Now I had nothing to do
but wait. The tow truck would arrive shortly. Maybe I could
persuade the driver to give me a ride to Aurora Pond before

he turned around to take the Volvo to the impound yard, but, if not, the dawn had to arrive sooner or later, and somewhere down the road—I had forgotten to ask exactly how far—lay the lapping waters of Aurora Pond. Jeff's sweater felt good and I was wearing a pair of sturdy shoes. The wild dogs seemed to have disappeared. The night had gotten warmer.

I opened the automatic window a crack to breathe in the night air and watched the interior lights grow dim. I closed the window. The lights grew dimmer. *No wonder Muriel had been driving without her headlights*, I thought—she must have been trying to save her battery.

The lights went completely off. My heart started to race until I remembered the penlight I'd won at the Rainbow Lanes. I took it out of my pocket, felt for the switch along the side, and pushed it forward. Out shot a small but steady beam; not much, but enough. I could feel my heart begin to slow again.

I sat in the car, shining the penlight here and there—sometimes on the turban, sometimes at the miniature white plastic door affixed to her dashboard. It was complete with a tiny golden doorknob, and on its base was written the words *Step On Through*, evidently the motto of the fellowship. I shined the penlight through the window and looked outside. There was no moon, but the asphalt of the road's surface sparkled slightly in its beam. I could stay in the car and wait, or I could step on through, using the light to keep me on the road. I thought about it. There was no guarantee the truck would arrive that night; dawn would be arriving soon. Why not walk and get a head start on things?

Never in my entire life had I taken a stroll in pitch darkness down a narrow country road away from the glow of the city, listening to the scratching of crickets, to the barking of farm dogs carried on the thick night air, to the sounds of gravel crunching satisfyingly beneath my feet, along with the scrunch of an occasional stepped-on empty beverage can, all the while imagining far above my head the silent, invisible, indifferent, pensive spiral of the stars. Outside of what was illuminated by the narrow beam of the penlight I could see nothing, but I could hear the sounds of nature herself, the same sounds I supposed that had existed back before the depredations of man, back during those great days of the ancient Greeks, and even earlier.

I walked on. My right foot entered a puddle the beam had failed to warn me of and my shoe got wet, but after a short time it dried out again, mostly. Once in a while I heard overhead the distant roar of an airplane and looked up to see it marked by its lights, ferrying a load of passengers away from Cleveland, the same trip soon that awaited me. I had forgotten to wear a watch. Time, that old fooler, expanded and compressed itself, rolled over and played dead, only to spring back to life again when I least expected it. How long I walked, I couldn't tell. It could have been hours. It might have been minutes. I heard the high squeals of bats and the sharp cries of night birds. I heard my own breath grow heavy as I trudged up a smallish hill, then I heard it ease on the way down. The wild dogs, or a completely different set of wild dogs, were back.

At last I saw a large, square truck slow down in response to my more or less frantic gestures and pull off the road to wait. The words *Fresh Fish* were written on its rear door, and I lost no time jogging to the passenger side and climbing in.

"Thanks," I said. "I was getting a little chilly out there."

The driver stared ahead. "Happy to help," he said without, however, looking especially happy, and from then on he lapsed into a prolonged silence. He was wearing a scarf that covered most of his face, a thick overcoat, heavy gloves, and a fur hat, no doubt because the back of the truck was mostly full of ice to keep the fish from spoiling. In any case, the cab was cold and damp and fishy-smelling. I assumed his heater didn't work, or he'd surely be using it.

After about ten minutes he turned to me. "Where you headed?" he asked.

"Aurora Pond," I answered.

He grunted in satisfaction.

"Thanks," I said again. "I appreciate it." There was something about his voice—familiar or not familiar, I couldn't tell—that made me wonder what it would sound like without the muffling effect of the scarf he was speaking into. But I didn't have a chance to find out, because he relapsed into another silence that was even longer and deeper. He seemed intent on some inner train of thought I could not begin to fathom. After a while he turned on the radio and somehow found an endless stream of Sinatra, Basie, and Dinah Washington—music from a whole other century. Outside the cab it was dark except for the startled eyes of the occasional raccoon or opossum or wild cat, followed by a thump as the truck hurtled over them with its burden of dead fish.

"If you don't mind me asking," I asked, "where are you taking a load of fish at this time of night?"

The man leaned forward and shut off the radio. "If all you're going to do is talk," he said, "you'd better leave now."

"What?"

"I said get out. Now. You're there."

He slowed the truck to a stop and motioned toward the door. I opened it. It was only a little colder outside than in the cab of the truck. Aurora Pond or not, there was a scary tone to his voice that made it seem as if he could turn violent at any second.

"Sure. Yes. You're the boss," I said, and exited.

He pulled the truck back onto the road without another word, and I watched the taillights disappear around a curve. The smell of fish began to dissipate in the moist night air. Where the truck had stopped to let me out the ground was soaked as if the truck had been leaking—melted ice, I guessed. I took a few tentative steps into the darkness. Just ahead of me, faintly at first, but ever more clearly, I could hear the sounds of nature's own plunger working away in some clogged toilet: the basso chunk-a-chunk of the giant bullfrogs that inhabited the weed-clogged circumference of Aurora Pond.

It's true there wasn't a moon but I did not need a moon to locate Sarge's Baits, whose stench of rotten crayfish, red worms, and dead minnows smoldered in the darkness of the night like a glowing hunk of ancient Limburger. There were no police guards—why should there be? There was nothing worth stealing. Shining the light on the dirt path to the shack, I pushed through the yellow police tape, found the heavy wooden door to the bait shack and opened it. Even before I could shine the penlight around I knew I had made a mistake. My eyes watered, my throat seized up, and I could not breathe. Nothing could possibly live in there, and if it did, related to me or not, I didn't ever want to meet it. I shut the door quickly and walked, choking a bit, toward the pond.

It was dark, so dark I could barely see my own elbow, let alone my hand in front of me but, using the penlight as a guide, I made my way to the small waves lapping against the dock where the faithful rowboats still waited in vain for customers. I inched forward onto the dock's wet and slippery planks.

At the dock's end I sat and splashed a little of the pond's icy water onto my face, as much to wash away the stink of the bait shack as for any other reason, and it was then that three things occurred to me: First, it was too dark to see my own face in the water, let alone anything else, and if I kept stumbling around alone in this complete darkness I could well kill myself. Second, if I got into one of the rowboats and sculled around the pond for a bit, I probably would not come to any harm and would be safe from the wild dogs. Last, for all I knew, this creature I was supposed to find— my half brother—might actually *be* somewhere out there on the pond doing whatever it was Zero did.

I crawled into one of the boats, untied it, and pushed off from the dock with a weighty oar. Then I began to row, awkwardly, unevenly at first, as it had been many years since the summer camp Linda had sent me to for three months when she had been called away to, as she said, "pay her dues." It was a place where the counselors had tied me to a massive wooden compost bin and left me there one afternoon as a joke, a place where I and the other children had first learned to row a leaky raft across a shallow bay. Camp Whispering Pines. Now I headed out to what I could only guess was the center of the pond. I faced the shore, toward the stern, but it was so dark it didn't really make a difference because I couldn't see where I was going anyway. Eventually I got into a kind of rhythm: lift, bend, down, pull. It felt good. The exercise was warming and Aurora Pond felt infinite. I would join a gym with a rowing machine when I returned to St. Nils, I decided, but at that moment I felt free from everything: free from the pressures of the gardening implement business, from the competition of the world of art, and even, in a way, from the promise I had made my mother. I was where I was supposed to be. Then all at once I felt very tired, more tired in fact than I could ever remember having been in my entire life.

I let the oars hang in the water and leaned back. Someone had left a life cushion in the boat. It had been tucked under a seat, shielded from the dew, so it was still dry. I put it behind my neck to use as a pillow. The slight mist on my face was not uncomfortable, and the night, except for the sounds around me, was still. I felt warmer, possibly the result of the water retaining the day's heat. On the highway that ran by the pond I could hear the mournful whine of a car or a truck, maybe a sixteen-wheeler, taking cattle to one of the nearby slaughterhouses.

The black air smelled of mud and plants and rotting bait.

An owl sounded from behind me—perhaps I was closer to the opposite shore than I'd guessed.

I remembered once again my mother's last request.

"OK, Mom, I'll give it a try," I said under my breath. "Here goes.

"Hey," I whispered off the right side of the boat. "Hey."

I don't know what I'd expected—actually nothing in particular, I suppose—but in any case there was no reply.

I switched to the left side. "Hey," I said again. "Zero." All at once this whole enterprise seemed absurd.

Who was this so-called brother of mine and what exactly was I supposed to tell him? I tried to remember so that if he came up suddenly out of the pond I wouldn't be at a loss for words. Something about eating right and being brave, that he was my long-lost brother, and that he wouldn't be seeing his mom for a while? I felt as if I were waking slowly from a dream—no, an enchantment that had been laid upon me, maybe at my birth, by an unknown godmother who'd been miffed over some imagined insult. And my punishment was that I had to grow up without a real mom. Zero, after all, had had *his*. On the other hand, maybe what I had thought was a punishment had actually been a gift, and when my mother left and for a long while afterward I'd been too young to tell the difference between a curse and a blessing.

"Zero," I said again softly, but this time I didn't bother to turn either to the right or to the left. I would wait until it got light, I decided, and then row back to shore and catch a ride to town, where I would have to tell the police that I'd seen my mother, or at least had heard from her. If this being-dead business was a trick on her part, which it could easily have been, come to think of it, then she'd probably wind up doing serious time in prison, maybe even the same one that had held Uleene. Anyway, by then I thought that the police probably would have gotten wind of the whole bowling alley affair themselves, so I didn't feel particularly guilty. I had forgiven my mother for everything she had done and everything she hadn't done for me, but I had to admit that the facts of the case didn't play out in her favor. After I filed whatever kind of report was necessary with the police, I'd be on the next plane back to St. Nils.

Then, out in front of my boat, I heard a small splashing sound in the water. Did Aurora Pond have muskrats? Would a pack of wild dogs swim up to a boat in order to attack its passenger? I doubted it, but come to think of it, I had no real idea of what kind of wildlife inhabited these parts or how exactly it could be expected to behave. Surely, Ohio was much too far north to support alligators.

I lifted my head to look out over the edge of the boat, holding the penlight above the dark water to see if I could determine the source of the noise. Alas, its beam only projected about six feet, and then, worst of all, when I tried to transfer it to my other hand, I watched it fall with a barely audible plop into the water, gleam downward for a foot or two, and then go out.

I was alone in the dark in a boat with something I did not know swimming around me.

Seemingly of its own accord, the prow of the boat swung around and began to surge forward even as my oars hung in the water and my hands stayed folded in my lap. I thought briefly about pulling the oars back into the boat and picking one up to use as a weapon to protect myself, but they were heavy and awkward and covered with slime. I could barely lift one of them out of the water, let alone wield it as a club in an already unsteady boat. I guessed that I could take hold of the anchor and toss it over the side to slow the boat down, but then I'd be stuck out there in the middle of the pond with who or whatever was pulling the boat forward as if it were a toy. That didn't seem like such a good idea, either.

I could scream, but even if anyone heard me there would be no possible way to find me in the pitch-black night. Plus, my scream would tell whatever it was out there exactly where I could be found. Though I guessed it already knew.

And then . . .

I was in the dark.

With nothing that could help me.

And . . .

And then I twisted and raised myself up on one elbow to see something ahead of me—not really see, of course, because it was so completely, terrifyingly, and mind-numbingly dark—but in that one molecule of my mind that was not completely numb, I saw what I supposed must have been a kind of vision: a door, no longer miniature, but full-sized, made of light-colored oak, with a brass knob in the shape of an oval on the right side, where I could grab it—a matching brass knocker, too—and lying there in front of the door was a doormat with the words *Step On Through* printed in bristles of a different color.

I lay my head back on the pillow and kept my eyes shut as tightly as I could. OK, I thought. I could take that step;

I *would* take the first step by ceasing to fear. I would let this thing, whatever it was, take me wherever it was going. First I would save my energy, and then when the situation became clear I would decide what I was going to do to save myself, but whether it was because Aurora Pond was *a lot* bigger than I'd guessed, or because we were going in circles, the trip was lasting far longer than I would have thought possible.

I lay there, my breath shallow, my heart racing, feeling the boat being pulled through the water, and wondering what was coming next. And then, because a person can only press his eyes shut hard for so long, bit by bit, I let them relax, and maybe I dozed off, or maybe I didn't, but when at last I opened my eyes the boat was continuing to move through the fog and the sky was starting to get light, although it still wasn't possible to see the shore very clearly because a layer of thick morning mist covered everything.

Then I felt a bump, followed by the scraping sound of the rowboat being pulled up, or maybe—come to think of it—*pushed* onto the shore, but whether I had come to an island (and I certainly didn't remember that Aurora Pond had any islands) or the far shore (because the smell of the bait house had grown markedly more faint), I couldn't tell. So then it was clear I could see the boat *was* being pushed, and, even as I was pondering the answer to the question of who or what was doing the pushing, I sat up and saw behind me something the color of the water, but as large as a bear, with a gleaming brown wet pelt like a bear's also, rise slowly up from the pond. And although its hands were webbed and its face was not the least bearlike but more human—flat, albeit without a nose and with several long black whiskers, like an otter's or a catfish's—the look on its face was surprisingly sweet all in all. So in the end this thing nudged my craft up onto the shore as easily as a child would push a paper boat, and I noticed with a sigh of relief that whatever it was could not be entirely wild because then it would not have been wearing a pair of tattered khaki swim trunks, nor would it have had sticking out of its tiny wet ears, two blue earplugs.

"Private Zero," I gasped, but before he could reply (*could* he even reply?) my attention was drawn to the island—for it *was* an island, bare of vegetation, and as the mist evaporated I could see the shore, where a small crowd of people stood waving, welcoming me to what looked—to judge by the blankets laid out on the mud, and the baskets of food and potables, and a grill, too, for barbecuing, though it was still early in the day—very much like a picnic.

Raul and Ramon were among the people gathered there; I hadn't realized until I saw them together how very similar they looked. Close to them was Uleene, who must have finished with whatever business she had said she needed to take care of earlier, and next to her stood El Diablo, though how in the world she could have gotten that heavy motorcycle onto this tiny mudflat of an island was beyond me. And then, surprisingly, or maybe not surprisingly at all at that point, I saw my mother for the first time in a long time, standing quietly behind the three of them, looking very much the way she had when I had last seen her alive in her apartment above the Treasure Chest, a week or two before that last phone call. She looked tired and relaxed, and no longer worried-looking in the least. Next to her Frau Elise was whispering, but I couldn't tell if my mother was listening or not. And standing behind her was Doorperson Muriel, who must have escaped from police custody, because the handcuffs were still hanging from one wrist like a charm bracelet (except that if she'd escaped, how could I explain the fact that Officer Jeff was standing there right next to her, sipping from a cup of steaming coffee?). Also gathered nearby were some ladies from the women's clubs I'd visited, but who belonged to which club I couldn't remember, except for Mitzie from the Hot Club, who waved at me, and in addition there were also several strangers with startled expressions on their faces who were walking around in aimless circles with gardening implements poking into and out of various parts of their bodies, and even Sunshine had put in an appearance, standing off to one side and holding one of those sticks you use for shaping clay in one hand and her Louisville Slugger in the other. She must have taken the bat along, I guessed, in hopes that maybe the island would have water rats or something, and there were other people who looked familiar as well, but whom I couldn't place where or when I'd seen, though many of them whom I would have sworn were complete strangers seemed to know me—in any case they were feeding scraps of meat to the group of wild-looking dogs who waited patiently around them—and, most amazing of all, was Sarge, who was holding a can of Diet Sprite and who, despite the fact he clearly had been in the water a very long time and had five—no, I could see as he turned, six—bullet holes in him, one right through his neck, seemed otherwise cheerful and actually really glad to meet

MY THANKS to the early readers of this novel, Lee Montgomery and Monona Wali, for their timely suggestions, as well as Tony Perez of Tin House Books, Jenny Burman for her carfeul proofreading, and especially my editor, a great noticer of things, Meg Storey. As always, I am grateful for the support of my wife, Jenny.

PUBLIC LIBRARIES OF SAGINAW

3 1390 01397 2052

Fiction Krusoe
Krusoe, James.
Erased /

PUBLIC LIBRARIES OF SAGINAW
ZAUEL MEMORIAL LIBRARY
3100 N. CENTER
SAGINAW, MI 48603

GAYLORD